For Martin Clarke
and in memory
of Emilie

susan b.
kelly

New York London Toronto Sydney Tokyo Singapore

KID'S STUFF

CHARLES SCRIBNER'S SONS

CHARLES SCRIBNER'S SONS
Rockefeller Center
1230 Avenue of the Americas
New York, NY 10020

Designed by Songhee Kim

Manufactured in the United States of America

1 3 5 7 9 10 8 6 4 2

Library of Congress Cataloging-in-Publication Data

Kid's Stuff/Susan B. Kelly
p. cm.
1. Trevellyan, Nick (Fictitious character)—Fiction.
2. Police—England—West Country—Fiction.
3. West Country (England)—Fiction.
I. Title.
PR6061.E4965K5 1994   94-23285 CIP
823'.914—dc20

ISBN 0-684-19649-2

"The supply of potential victims seems inexhaustible. . . . Children used in pornography seem to come from every class, religion and family background. A majority are exploited by someone who knows them by virtue of his or her occupation or through a neighborhood, community or family relationship."

US Attorney General's Commission on Pornography, 1986

"English gentleman, 37, pedophile, wishes to meet a mother with Lolita daughter or lady with pedophile feelings with view to marriage."

Lolita *magazine, 1985*

Part One

Go practise if you please
With men and women: leave a child alone
For Christ's particular love's sake!

Robert Browning
The Ring and the Book

1

The bench was wooden and slatted and in the dark municipal green favored by the Hop Valley District Council. It was by no means new and had faded and blistered with the years, but it was still possible to make out that it was dedicated to the memory of Eric Duodecimus Penhaligon, who had died in 1954 and whose favorite spot this had been. The name gave Nick pause: could Eric really have been son number twelve—a whole Penhaligon cricket team with little Eric as twelfth man? If so, why wasn't the valley full of Penhaligons? He knew of only two or three in the town. Had their excessive fecundity spent itself in one generation?

Penhaligon wasn't strictly a local name either but came from farther south, from Cornwall, like his own family name of Trevellyan. It seemed that many Cornish families must have come drifting up that steep Atlantic coast over the centuries—seeking a milder landscape and warmer hearts.

Nick had plenty of time for these reflections. It was a slow day and a tranquil one where any movement seemed excessive. It was the hottest summer since 1976 and the longest: there had been no break in the weather since early

May and it was now mid-July. There were just a few wisps of white cloud in the sky today, the faintest of breezes bringing the smell of the rose garden to him. It was the sort of day when you didn't want to do anything except sit on a bench in a park, in the sun, in your shirtsleeves with a pretty girl.

Which was precisely what Detective Chief Inspector Nick Trevellyan was doing. He was sitting on Eric's bench in Riverside Park with Detective Constable Carol Halsgrove. He had his left arm round her and she was nuzzling against him. Any casual stroller in the park that day would have seen a plausible pair of lovers: a serious-looking man in his mid-thirties, slender, almost thin, in his blue jeans and plain grey cotton shirt, with unruly dark curls, tanned skin, gold-rimmed spectacles; taking a long lunch break with this slightly younger woman who was small, wiry, not immediately drawing the eye with her unremarkable brown hair, regular features and Marks and Spencer skirt and blouse; not beautiful, not at all, but with an interesting face and intelligent blue eyes.

Nick felt happy. He dropped a light kiss on Carol's forehead. She gave him an adoring look. "Good," he said. Carol began to giggle. She was an invaluable member of CID but once she got the giggles . . . Nick poked her in the ribs, hard. "Stop that! Or I'll have you on a disciplinary charge."

"Sorry." She buried her head in his shoulder, shaking, and put her hand on his knee to steady herself. "I was just remembering the look on Shirley's face when you said you and I would be on this bench and she and Paul could hang around by the boating pond."

"I don't trust you and Paul to keep your minds on your work."

"You mean you don't trust Shirley once she's got you at her mercy on a park bench." They both began to giggle.

"This is it," Nick said suddenly. "Here he comes." He took Carol in his arms and embraced her hard so that her head was looking over his shoulder and, between them, they had a clear view in both directions. A man came towards them from the School Road entrance, hurrying in the direction of the pond, not seeing, or not noticing, the young lovers on the bench.

Nick watched him through half-closed eyes, his mind automatically registering his description; ready to disseminate it to colleagues if necessary or recite it in court. The man was in his late thirties, of medium height, and had once been handsome but was now fading and running to fat. His hair was straight and thick, needed tidying, slightly greasy and very black; his skin the olive of warmer climates. Black eyes topped a broad nose, fleshy mouth and sharp chin.

"That's him all right," Nick said.

He had to be the only person in the park that day wearing a jacket which he held tightly closed with his fingers as he moved. It bulged slightly in front with the weight of a package or parcel. It made him uncomfortably hot, and beads of sweat broke unpleasantly on his forehead.

"He's heading for the boathouse," Carol whispered, "like you thought."

When he had passed them, they got up and walked after him, entwined in each other's arms. Detective Constable Paul Penruan and Woman Detective Sergeant Shirley Walpole were standing together feeding a couple of uninterested mallards. He was tall and handsome and casually elegant, she the vivacious girl next door—newlyweds, perhaps, discussing the future. They were holding hands but not putting on half as good a show as Nick and Carol.

The dark man paused for breath and took out a large white handkerchief to wipe his sweating face. He glanced quickly about him, then walked round the pond and into the boathouse. It was half past twelve and Old Chalky, who hired out the boats, had just gone over to the Cross and Sparrow for a pint and a sandwich. You could set your watch by him, and keen boaters knew that they could get an extra half hour for their money if they timed it right.

"The client went in a couple of minutes ago," Shirley murmured in Nick's ear as he passed her. No one walking by would have heard more than the whisper of the breeze across the flowering magnolia branches.

Carol and Nick strolled along the same route as the black-eyed man, circling the pond anticlockwise. Paul and Shirley waited until they were well past, then began to walk round it in the other direction. Paul pointed at something in the distance, then hugged Shirley and gave her a kiss on the cheek. No one paid any attention to these two attractive couples taking the air on a fine summer's day. The four of them arrived at the boathouse at the same time, just as the dark man was coming out. Nick nodded.

Shirley and Paul charged into the boathouse. Nick took the dark man by the right arm with a feeling of warm satisfaction. This arrest was the culmination of weeks of preparatory work, of liaison with other forces. It could be about to fizzle out in embarrassment and threats of lawsuits for wrongful arrest, but he thought not.

"Arturo Bottone, I'm a police officer. I have a warrant for your arrest for the publication and distribution of obscene material contrary to the Protection of Children Act 1978."

Nick's hold on his arm was too firm for flight to be contemplated, and the man stood helplessly as he was cautioned, not speaking. Nick unbuttoned the bulky jacket and removed a white envelope from the inside pocket. Shirley came out of the boathouse with another man in her equally hard grip, Paul following behind with a brown paper parcel tucked under his arm. The parcel was foolscap size, two inches thick, and a tear in one corner showed that it was made up mostly of magazines.

"It was in his briefcase," Paul said.

The second man began to bluster. He was a jittery little creature of about forty with thinning hair and a black leather briefcase which he held protectively across his front with one hand. He was the prosperous businessman in his lightweight summer suit—the jacket hooked by one finger over his shoulder—and short-sleeved shirt. Circles of sweat were clearly visible under his armpits. His sallow cheeks were flushed, and his voice rose in anger and fear to a squeak.

"This is preposterous. I have no idea what this young woman is talking about. I was feeling a little faint and went into the boathouse to get out of the sun for a minute. Then these two people burst in and assaulted me, claiming to be police officers. It's outrageous."

"Mr. Tyson," Nick said. "Our friendly local insurance broker." He took the parcel from Paul, tore it open a little farther, examined the topmost magazine. "*Nudist Moppets.* How delightful—" He felt down between the magazines and pulled a handful of black-and-white photographs out at random.

Shirley, glancing at the top one, seeing a dazed child flinching in fear, let out an exclamation of disgust.

"And I suppose Mr. Bottone just happened to come in while you were resting," Nick continued, "and just happened to leave this parcel in your briefcase, and you just happened to give him this envelope containing"—he lifted the flap of the envelope he had taken from Bottone and riffled through the wad of five-pound notes—"about eighty quid, by the look of it."

"I don't sell the stuff," Tyson whined. "It was him. He's the dealer."

"Nice try, Mr. Tyson, but I'm afraid it's illegal just to buy it, just to have it in your possession. Maximum penalty, two years." Tyson gasped and his lips mouthed "Two years!" without any sound coming out.

"Wesley Tyson," Nick went on, "I am arresting you for possession of this pornographic material contrary to the Criminal Justice Act of 1988. You are not obliged to say anything, but anything you say may be given in evidence. Carol, get the other bit moving."

Carol conjured a shortwave radio from somewhere under her loose cotton blouse and spoke into it. "Inspector Burcombe from WDC Halsgrove. Receiving. Over."

The radio responded; a rough male voice said, "Go ahead, Carrie."

"Message from DCI Trevellyan. We've made our arrest and you're to proceed with your entry and search at the address provided at once, repeat, at once. Over."

"Consider it done. Out."

"I want to speak to my solicitor," Tyson said.

"You will do," Nick told him. "Back at the station. You can talk to your solicitor and to Mrs. Tyson."

2

Inspector Colin Burcombe walked into Nick's office four hours later; as usual, he didn't bother to knock. Nick glanced up from the report he was writing on their day's work and frowned. His relationship with Burcombe was an uneasy one, but he was dependent on him and his uniformed PCs for backup, and he put a lot more effort into making it work than Colin ever did.

Burcombe was a little older than Nick, although below him in the hierarchy. The inspector had come up through the ranks, the hard way, slowly, over a period of almost twenty years, and would never now make Chief Inspector. There was a simmering resentment about him which alarmed Nick. His work had coarsened him and left him cynical.

He had a cigarette in his mouth, and Nick handed him an ashtray without a word. He scowled, stubbed the cigarette out, threw himself into the empty chair on the other side of the desk and folded his arms. He was taller and heavier than Nick, had receding brown hair which he kept very short like the smooth pelt of some small animal, hard eyes, a mean mouth, an ex-fighter's nose. Today he was in plainclothes: an aging pinstriped suit pulled out of shape by overladen pockets. The suit made him look thuggish in a way that more casual clothes could not have done; he wore a tight black T-shirt beneath it outlining the firm pectoral muscles he was so proud of.

He pulled a packet about the size of a large-format paperback book out of his right pocket and tossed it on the desk. Nick picked it up. It was a VHS videotape—not a commercial tape but one which had originally been sold as a blank for home use. Someone had scrawled two words in ballpoint on the spine.

"*Loving Daddy,*" Nick read out.

"We've just been running it through the VCR downstairs in the recreation room," Burcombe said. "It's the real thing. Want to take a look?"

"Thank you, no. I can imagine."

Burcombe leered slightly. "Yeah?" He picked up one of Bottone's magazines from the pile on the corner of Nick's desk and began to leaf through it. Nick reached across and took it from him. He put the whole pile into his desk drawer and locked it. "Share and share alike," Burcombe said, "only fair."

"You don't suppose I like looking at this filth?" Nick asked.

Burcombe shrugged. "Boys will be boys."

"Is that all you got at Colt's Head?"

"That's just a sample. There are another dozen videos although some of them are duplicates, judging by the labeling. We've also got a pile of magazines this high—" he demonstrated "and some glossy black-and-white photos. Very artistic."

In a sense he was right, Nick thought. One of the notable things about the photographs was, as you might say, how *good* they were. It needed talent to set the exposure just right, so that the tears falling from a little girl's tired eyes were caught suspended in midair like monochrome bubbles; it took practice and skill.

"I want it all up here," he said, "in my safekeeping. Okay?"

"Sir," Burcombe said sulkily.

"Where did he keep it?"

"Out in the stables, funnily enough. I gather he and his missus—tasty bird but a bit stuck up—don't share a room. He sleeps in a place above the stalls which used to be a hayloft. There's a camp bed in it now and a chest of drawers. This stuff was in the bottom drawer." He grinned. "Talk about don't frighten the horses, eh? Of course, they're all sex mad, these eyeties. Well known fact. It's the climate."

"And was the list there too?"

"Ah. I was coming to that."

"You got the list of names and addresses? His customers, contacts?"

"I swear, Nick, we turned the place upside down, inside out, and back to front. All I found was an address book belonging to his missus which obviously wasn't it."

"Why not?"

"It was mostly women in there, and all over the place—London, Surrey. Hardly any local at all. Lady This and Sir Somebody Something. Racehorse trainers, stewards; posh people. I brought it in all the same but it's no good."

"Shit." Nick got up, went to the window, turned back, sat down again, fidgeted with his telephone. "That was what I wanted more than anything."

"You've got him, Bottone."

11

"Big deal! So I send him away for a short stretch, couple of years maximum. What do his suppliers and customers do? Find themselves another middle man. Back to square one."

Inspector Burcombe's resentment, which had been bubbling steadily for the past ten minutes, boiled over. "Now look, we even sifted through the straw in the stalls, and mighty shitty some of it was, I can tell you. And another thing, I'm not keen on horses, bloody great brutes. I should get danger money. You don't believe us, you go and look for yourself."

"I'm not doubting your thoroughness, Colin. But there must have been a list at some stage. He was dealing in this stuff on a big scale. He can't just have memorized all the names and addresses."

"Looks like he saw us coming then."

"What!"

"He had advance warning, got shut of it."

"Then why did he turn up at Riverside Park to be arrested?"

"Well, someone at the stables had advance warning then, burned it while Bottone was out being nicked."

"Who knew about this?"

"I had six men on the job."

"But you didn't need to give them details. I gave you clear instructions to keep it under your hat."

"My blokes aren't daft, even if they're not CID. They had an inkling of what it was about; people talk."

"Yes," Nick said meaningfully, "don't they just. Especially after a couple of large scotches."

"Now look here—" Burcombe started to rise to his feet.

"All right, all right." Nick backed away, as usual, from

outright confrontation, and the other man slowly resumed his seat, satisfied of victory. "You searched the house as well as the stables?"

"Course. By the way, I asked his missus if she wanted to come down and bail him out, and she said a night in the cells wouldn't hurt him." Burcombe smiled icily. "Ain't love grand?"

"He'll be spending a night in the cells whether she comes down or not."

"You're not bailing him then?"

"He's a foreign national."

"I've got his passport."

"Even so. I shall be asking the magistrates to remand him in custody in the morning."

"It's not like it's murder or something," Burcombe said.

"Tyson's been charged and bailed, except that I gather Mrs. Tyson won't let him back in the house."

"He's not getting any more business from me."

"Is there anyone still there now, at the stables?"

"No. We've packed up and gone home. And don't forget you authorized the overtime."

"I'm not likely to. Okay." Nick offered an olive branch. "You did your best. Thank you. We'll have to hope Bottone can remember a few names."

"Have you charged him?"

"Not yet. Shirley and Paul are still talking to him." He got up. "I'll go down and have a word."

Burcombe also rose. "I'll be off home myself then."

"Not until you've brought me up the rest of the videos and magazines," Nick reminded him. The inspector started to leave the room without replying. "Did you hear me, Colin? I'm not having them lying around the evidence cupboard for anyone to pick up. They're hard-core porn and policemen have no more moral right to look at them than Tyson has. Less."

"I expect you'll be having a good peek yourself," Burcombe said, "sir."

"No more than I have to." Nick didn't add that the first two he had glanced through had sickened him; Burcombe would take that as an admission of weakness. "We've put a lot of work into this," he said instead, "and I want a good result."

"Me too. I've got two little girls of my own, remember. Mind you, I haven't seen them for four years and probably wouldn't recognize them if I fell over them in the street." Nick mumbled a half-hearted condolence—he wasn't convinced that Colin Burcombe was a good male role model for two suggestible little girls—but Burcombe brushed the words aside. "Oh, they've got a stepfather, an accountant—earns a lot more than me and is home evenings and weekends. They don't need me and I don't need your sympathy. G'night."

He left and Nick sighed. They had rapidly got onto the wrong foot, as usual. There seemed no help for it. There had been too many cases over the years of policemen throwing parties to cackle over the pornographic films they had confiscated and smoke the dope they had found in some kid's pocket; and those were just the ones that reached his ears. Burcombe was not going to go down that road this time, not if Nick could help it.

Interview Room One had the usual notice up about not going in while the red light was on. The red light was on, but Nick went in anyway. Shirley looked up crossly and he smiled an apology. She said into the tape recorder: "DCI Trevellyan enters the room at"—she glanced up at the clock on the far wall—"1712."

He took a seat to one side and listened for a few minutes while Shirley and Paul took it in turns to ask Bottone questions. The man had refused an interpreter and his English was fluent and only lightly accented although with the overemphatic inflections of the native Italian speaker. He showed no contrition, lounged in his chair as comfortably as if he'd been in his own sitting room, nibbled his fingernails at intervals. He had yet to give a straight answer to a straight question and looked as if he had nothing better to do this summer's evening than sit in conversation with this charming woman sergeant and this personable young constable.

His solicitor sat stiffly by his side, looking as if he would rather be somewhere else, jotting the odd note. He was Derek Collins, of Waters and Collins, one of the duty solicitors. He was a plain man in his late thirties, his lank, fair hair and plump face unmemorable. He knew this bare, windowless room well, visited it several times a month, never got to like it any better. He found it claustrophobic and overhot even in the depths of winter; on a day like this it was stifling. He had not come across a case of this sort before—petty theft was more his line—and he was running his finger round the inside of his collar, finding it too tight.

Finally Shirley came to a halt. She had asked Bottone the same questions several times; he had been polite and courteous and had made no real answer at all. She glanced a query at Nick.

"Mr. Bottone," Nick said, getting up and approaching

the table, "did you have a list of customers for your pornographic magazines and videos?"

"List?" He shrugged. "I don't really have *customers,* just keep it for my own consumption and a few good friends. Get it?"

"The amount of goods seized at your stables this afternoon indicates rather more than a peep show for a few mates."

"So, I have a lot of friends." He smiled a whore's smile at Nick. His teeth were small and yellowish and regular. "Arturo Bottone is a very popular chap."

"I'll bet. And you didn't write down the names and addresses of any of these pals of yours?"

"I have a good memory."

"Excellent. Then you can dictate a few names to the sergeant to be going on with."

Bottone was silent for a moment, then he said reasonably, "Look, I know the score. You send me away for a little while for having these magazines. Okay. Suppose I tell you who my friends are; you still send me away and I have no friends left when I come back. It doesn't make sense. Get it?"

"Your cooperation can be taken into account by the Crown Court when they sentence you."

He looked at his solicitor. "This is true?"

"I suppose with a guilty plea, the judge might be inclined to leniency but—"

Bottone interrupted. "How long can you send me away for anyway? A few months? I can do that. My friends are important men, they easily get upset. Get it?"

"I'm an important man," Nick said, "and I get upset very easily, especially when I see small children being hurt and degraded for the pleasure of a handful of perverts."

Bottone spread his arms wide. "More like an armful."

He laughed at his own wit.

"Am I to understand, Chief Inspector," the solicitor said, "that further examples of"—he picked up the magazine the detectives had brought into the interview room with them and held it between thumb and forefinger with distaste—"*this* have been found on my client's premises?"

"I don't say I don't have it," Bottone said.

"And possession of this material, as you are aware, Mr. Collins, is enough for me to hold him on."

"We shall be pleading not guilty to any further charge," Collins said promptly. "Of handling with intent to sell, that sort of thing."

"Charge him," Nick said to Shirley, "with possessing the stuff *and* with dealing in it."

"What sort of sicko wants to buy that muck anyway?" Derek Collins muttered to Nick as they filed into the charge room a few minutes later.

"Important men," Nick replied. "Apparently."

3

After supper that evening Nick and Alison sat in the drawing room at Hope Cottage sipping coffee. A slight breeze tweaked the curtains through the open French windows. Neither of them spoke, each following a train of private thought. No television or CD player interrupted their peace. The summer was the noisiest time of the year, Nick thought, with radios blaring through open car windows, the hum of lawn mowers, and birds and insects making whoopee; it increased the cool stillness of indoors.

To the disinterested observer, they made a less congruous couple than Nick and Carol had in the park that afternoon. Alison was a tall woman, not much under Nick's own five feet ten inches, and she was big-boned, though lean. She had an impressive amount of red hair, which fell almost to her waist while loose but which was tidied away now in a wispy bun at her nape. She had a large oval face with a rather long nose and clear green eyes which missed little. By day, when she was the managing director of Hope Software, her features shouted strength and determination; tonight, work put aside for the evening, her face was in repose and whispered calm contentment.

She went out after a while to brew a fresh pot. When she got back, the room was empty, Nick was gone; but she could see spotlights beginning to come on in the garden, flooding trees and shrubs and lawns with halogen light. She went out on the terrace and looked into the dusk. He was lying under the pear tree, stretched out on his back on the grass, not moving. She walked over to him. He was watching the constellations beginning to form in the clear sky: Orion with his sparkling belt, the Plough; Castor and Pollux, those twin souls.

"I was hoping you would come and join me." He shifted his gaze onto her.

"You'll catch your death," she told him. She could be prosaic.

"It's as warm and dry as can be." He patted the grass beside him. "Why don't you try it?"

"Are you thinking what I think you're thinking?"

"I think so."

"Then let me go and get a blanket at least."

"Okay, but hurry up or I shall start without you." He began to remove his shirt. Nothing overlooked the garden. Hope Cottage stood in its own grounds, slightly outside the village of Little Hopford, and they could be as sure of privacy in their garden as in their bedroom.

Alison returned in five minutes with two tartan blankets. "One to put over us later."

"We shan't be cold. Hurry up."

"What's got into you tonight?"

He didn't answer, didn't tell her why he wanted her so urgently; why he wanted a beautiful naked woman—a real one, with breasts and curved hips and pubic hair. To drive away the memory of those skinny pouting girl children.

She laid one blanket on the grass beside him, and he rolled over onto it and held a hand up to her. She pulled her thin cotton dress over her head, threw it to one side and joined him on the ground. He took two pins out of her bun, and the hair descended with a static crackle over both their shoulders. The breeze freshened and the smell of the pear tree, with its sweetly sexual scent, floated over them.

His hand ran down her rib cage as gently as the wings of a moth, coming to rest on her slightly concave belly. "There's nothing so delicious as this," he breathed into her ear, "making love in the open air on a perfumed summer's night, with—"

Just at that moment an image forced its way into his unwilling mind—one of the most disturbing of the many he had been forced to look at that afternoon. A little girl of about four or five captured with a fat man, and a woman who appeared, by the similarity of the features—the slightly slavic cast to the eyes, the flat nose, the pale skin—to be her mother. The man's face was out of shot, but the woman was smiling encouragement at the obviously drugged child, revealing a mundane glimpse of a gap tooth. The short text—full of capital letters and exclamation marks—had been in Danish; Nick had neither understood nor wished to.

"Oh no," he moaned.

Nudist Moppets, Lolitots, Bambinas: all those sickeningly cutesy titles. Then there were the mail-order advertisements for further magazines, videos: "See small girl romping with her uncles; black girl treated nasty." There was something peculiarly unpleasant in the precision of that semicolon. All desire left him. He rolled over away from her. "Sorry."

He explained as best he could, and Alison said, "Don't worry."

A swarm of gnats formed a mobile, translucent ball above them, eager for her peaches-and-cream legs, his honey-brown arms. He let out a little laugh, seeing the reality of this open-air lovemaking which was so different from his imaginings. He gave a little shiver, although it was still warm, as the long day's sweat dried on his body. She pulled the second blanket over them both and lay there for a while, just holding him against her.

When Nick woke the following morning, somebody had filled his head with cotton wool during the night and then sandpapered his throat. His temperature was 101. He was furious. Alison was concerned but not very sympathetic.

"I told you you'd catch your death," she pointed out.

"Colds are caused by viruses," Nick protested, "not by hanging around in the garden without your vest."

"The virus must have been lurking under that pear tree then," she said, "waiting for you."

"It's not as if anything came of it," he grumbled.

"Nor *anyone*," she agreed.

She consulted *Pears Medical Encyclopedia,* a book which met with her approval on the grounds that it recommended whisky for colds and flu. She mixed up a large shot of Bell's with some honey, lemon and hot water and brought it up to him.

"Ugh, God! Not first thing in the morning," he objected hoarsely.

"Suit yourself." She sat down on the end of the bed and began to sip the concoction herself. "Waste not, want not."

She refused to let him go to work, and he had to admit that his brain was not firing on all cylinders. He telephoned Shirley at home and issued a series of instructions about the appearances of Bottone and Tyson before the magistrates that morning. "It should all be quite straightforward," he said, "but ring me if you get into difficulties."

21

So he was surprised when, early that afternoon, Alison came up to the bedroom and said that Shirley was there and wanted a word. He said to send her up. Alison brought her up and stayed, not trusting Shirley not to climb into bed with Nick the minute her back was turned. Shirley looked in awe at Alison's huge, canopied bed.

"Welcome to the Sun King's levée," Nick said. "Everything go off okay? Get them remanded?"

"Tyson asked to be tried by the magistrates, which they agreed to. He pleaded guilty and they gave him a £200 fine and publicly slapped his wrists for him."

Nick made an exasperated noise. "Typical! Why couldn't they have sent him up for trial by jury and a proper sentence?"

"It's all very well talking about two years out in the park. You didn't really think any magistrate was going to send him down just for buying kiddy porn, did you?"

"The magistrates seem to think this sort of pornography is a harmless outlet. The sentences handed out are derisory. Okay. It can't be helped. What about Bottone?"

"Bottone's been committed for trial at the Crown Court next month—"

"Good."

"—on bail."

"What!" Nick croaked, hurting his raw throat.

Shirley looked round at Alison for moral support, but she was looking in the wrong place. "It was Dr. Wilberforce," she said feebly. "You know what he's like. And Mr. Collins was unexpectedly convincing."

"Damn!" Nick said. "I thought Mrs. Hanger-and-Flogger Fergusson was on this morning, not Dr. Wilberforce. I was planning to exercise all my charm on her."

"Mrs. Fergusson broke her arm out riding on Sunday," Shirley snapped. "And Dr. Wilberforce appears to be impervious to my charms." Alison looked unsurprised.

"A foreign national, though," Nick said. "That's a bit thick even for Wilberforce."

"He's lived round here ten years," she said, "as Collins was at great pains to point out. He's got a wife and a whole pack of kids and a business. He's not going running off. And we've got his passport."

"All right, Shirley. I expect you did your best." Nick dismissed her with a nod. She muttered that she hoped he would soon be better and Alison saw her out.

Bottone didn't need his passport to get where he was going, as it turned out. What Gerald Wilberforce, Ph.D., JP, said the next morning—or whenever it was he heard that Arturo Bottone had hanged himself in his own stables that night—has not been recorded.

Nick's body temperature was down below a hundred, unlike his temper, which was near boiling point.

"If only he'd given me those names!" he yelled at Alison when she brought him up some tea and aspirin and this unwelcome news. "If only the stupid bloody man had given me those names, this would never have happened. There'd've been no point."

"Why would giving you a set of names have stopped him committing suicide?" Alison asked, baffled.

"Suicide! Forget it. No one's going to convince me this was suicide." He got out of bed, told Alison rudely to stop fussing, showered, dressed and went to work.

4

Nick turned his car up the hill, heading for the moorland stables. The road was narrow and steep and ill-made, but he drove quite fast, adrenalin communicating itself to the accelerator.

He had recently bought a new—to him—car, a Peugeot 205, from his cousin Kit who had started dealing in used cars. He had done this against his better judgment, since he didn't trust Kit to distinguish a bargain from a rusty wheelbarrow, but the car had, to his astonishment, proved totally reliable in the four months it had been in his possession.

It handled well now on the curving road, and the brakes responded equally effectively when he rounded the next corner and came bumper to bumper with an ambulance. He maneuvred back into a passing place, and the driver gave him a wave of thanks and recognition before chugging on down. He began to pull out again, then spotted Shirley Walpole's little white Austin Metro also making its way carefully down the hill towards him. He stayed where he was and waited for her. She drew level with him; both of them had their windows open, since the heat was already building up, and she hailed him.

"Shouldn't you be in bed?"

"I take it Bottone was in that ambulance?"

"You take it right. I've got a statement from his wife, and the Scene of Crime team are going over the place. I was just coming over to Hope Cottage to report to you but I see you've heard."

"What's your view?"

"No sign of foul play. He was hanging from a rafter by a long rein—I think they call it a lunge rein. It was a thin leather thong and dug a deep furrow into his neck. There were no other signs of violence."

"Who found him?"

"The wife."

"You're not bringing her in?"

"I couldn't see any reason to at the moment."

"You're assuming suicide?"

"Yes." She had obviously thought the matter through, and Nick's confidence waned slightly; he trusted Shirley's judgment. "The scene was just right," she explained. "You know? A wooden chair kicked over; everything else left neat and tidy. Why do suicides always do that? I once knew a woman who springcleaned the house from top to bottom before going out and—"

"Note?" Nick interrupted.

"Well, no. But not everybody wants their famous last words recorded."

"Footprints?"

"Straw underfoot where it wasn't cobblestones. But the SOCOs will go on trying. I was on my way back to the office. Do you want me to come back to the stables with you?"

Nick sighed. His head was aching and he still felt a little feverish. He wished he'd taken those aspirins now. Suddenly it didn't seem worth the effort. "No. I'll come back to the office with you."

"You don't want to see for yourself, talk to Mrs. Bottone?"

"Eventually. Let's get the postmortem done first."

"See you down there, then."

She eased her car into gear and moved smoothly off. Nick carried on up to the next viewpoint where there was room to turn round. He sat there for a moment, switched off his engine, loosened his seat belt. The moors were silent, apart from the distant complaining of sheep and— even farther off—the drone of a light plane. Ahead of him, above, was the small hill named the Colt's Head which gave the stables its name; it had never looked anything like a horse's head to Nick. Behind him, below, lay the Hop Valley and, beyond that, the sea glittered in the sun.

Shirley was back at the station for almost half an hour before Nick appeared. She sat in his office waiting, keeping up a facade of activity, feeling sorry for herself. Yesterday he had criticized her, so unfairly, in front of the Hope woman. Today, Mrs. Bottone had spoken to her as if she were a servant. Who was she to be so snooty—the wife of a criminal pervert?

And the incident with Colin Burcombe in the canteen on Monday morning . . . she blushed at the memory.

"Don't mind him," Carol had whispered. "He thinks he's entitled to work his way through the female officers one by one."

But it wasn't that part that had rankled. It was that he had noticed, guessed her secret. And if an insensitive thug

26

like Burcombe had noticed, that meant everyone had.

Shirley took a small mirror out of the canvas rucksack she carried in preference to a handbag, and examined her face. She had deceptively soft features, concealing a burning ambition to storm her way to the top. It was a pleasant face with clear skin, deep-set brown eyes, a small, straight nose, a wide and generous mouth with a little mole at one corner which gave it a teasingly lopsided look. The whole was framed by tight dark curls which she kept short and bouncy, washed every morning and left to dry in the fresh air on the short walk to work. She knew she was pretty: men's eyes told her so. She was prettier than Alison Hope, surely, and, at twenty-eight, four years younger.

It was nine months since she had come to the Hop Valley—seconded from Headquarters as a temporary replacement for Sergeant Bill Deacon, who was undergoing major surgery. Temporary was a vague word, and this temporary had stretched and stretched and showed no sign of ending; nor was she sure if she wanted it to. But there were times when the insular manners of the valley—what she perceived as its small-mindedness and interference—got her down.

At those times she thought with longing of cities, of their anonymity: of Bristol, perhaps, or Exeter. In cities you could recreate yourself each day: a change of fashion, of make-up, of hair would make a different woman of you. Here, in Hopbridge, you would run into someone who knew you, who would ask what on earth you had done to your hair. Here you were the same old Shirley Walpole— neat and unexciting clothes, bare face—and if you didn't happen to like her today, that was just too bad.

There was London, even, a transfer to the Met—they

would snap her up with her experience. In London you didn't know your neighbor's name or what he did or even if he spoke English. People didn't pry. In London you could be in love with your boss and no one would care enough to notice and tease you. You wouldn't have to run into the woman he lived with three times a damn week and grit your teeth and be polite to her when all the time you wanted to pull her mess of coarse ginger hair and hear her squeal.

"No need to go mooning around after Trevellyan," Burcombe had called across to her in the canteen on Monday, making her face go all hot. "I'm available and mine's bigger."

"That's not what it says on the wall in the ladies'," Carol had retorted, wagging her little finger at Burcombe's table. The other men with Burcombe had roared with laughter and he had been silenced. Carol had then got up and cleared her tray away, saying, "Come on, Sarge. Let's leave these oafs to harass each other." Shirley had followed meekly, wondering why she could not come up with a putdown like that.

The door opened and Nick came in. He was carrying two polystyrene cups full of something that looked like steaming mud. "I wanted to say I was sorry about yesterday," he said. "I must have sounded as if I thought it was your fault. My only excuse is that I was feverish."

Shirley smiled and dismissed it with a wave of her hand. "I'm not so thin-skinned as that, Nick." In a way, his kindness made it worse. Catch many DCIs apologizing to their sergeants! He sat down and handed her one of the cups of coffee and began to sip from the other.

"What sort of woman is Mrs. Bottone?" he asked.

"Cool. Aloof. Not exactly heartbroken."

"You don't like her?"

"Not excessively. But I suppose I went there full of womanly sympathy and she wasn't having any of it. That's a bit galling."

"You felt rejected?"

"More or less." She laughed. "Daft, isn't it?"

"Give me the gist of her statement, will you?"

"Bottone came back to Colt's Head at about midday yesterday—must have come straight from the court. She wouldn't let him in the house, but it seems he mostly slept in the stables anyway. There's a sort of loft there set out as a bedsit."

"So I gathered from Colin."

"She didn't see him alive again. It looks as if he had a little private party that night, no shortage of empty bottles— Dutch courage, presumably. Got himself up to be just drunk enough to do it without a backward glance."

"And she found him, you say. When?"

"First thing. Six-thirtyish. They make an early start at riding stables, as she pointed out: mucking out, grooming—whatever they call it. It seems she mostly keeps her horses out in the paddock at this time of year, but there's one she keeps stabled—it's very valuable or very delicate or something. She was going to ride it herself that morning so came to fetch it from its stall and there he was, dangling."

"Did you get an estimate as to time of death from Dr. Brewster?"

"He was prepared to risk between midnight and four A.M."

"Hmm. What a mess. And it was all going so well."

"Saves us the cost of bringing him to court," she pointed out.

"Saves the skins of his important customers too."

"You're not happy, are you?"

"Not entirely. He wouldn't have got more than a couple of years for a first offense, if that. He might well have got off with a fine or a suspended, like Tyson. Why should he top himself?"

"Remorse?" Shirley hazarded.

"You saw how cocky he was in the interview room yesterday, smirking away. It was almost as if he thought some of those Important Men of his were going to extricate him from his trouble. Did that strike you as a man about to go home, get pissed and hang himself from the nearest rafter?"

"Maybe he realized suddenly that he'd lost his wife for good, earned the contempt of all right-thinking people. So he got drunk, the drink depressed him; it just happened that the means were there. A lot of people would kill themselves on the spur of the moment if they had the wherewithal handy."

"You reckon?" Nick asked, startled.

She blushed. "What I mean is that farmers have shotguns and doctors have cupboards full of drugs—that's why they have the top suicide rates of any profession. Farmer Giles suddenly thinks that it's not worth going on, so he gets out his shotgun and sticks it in his mouth. You or I feel down, think idly about how to do it, realize there's no easy way and soon cheer up again."

"Hanging's not an easy way."

"People think it is, though."

"So Bottone sees the rein lying there, the chair in his

bedsit, the rafter just waiting. . . . So very tempting, you think?"

"And he's done it before he's got time to think better of it, or write a note, or anything."

"Possible," Nick said.

"You're not buying it?"

"If only it weren't so convenient for all those Important Men. Who's to say they haven't extricated him in the most final way possible? Is Dr. Brewster doing the PM today?"

"He's giving a lecture in Bristol this afternoon. He'll do it tomorrow. Do you wanted it treated as a suspicious?"

"Not yet. No point in pulling the stops out and starting a murder hunt until we're sure."

Nick was feeling a lot better the following morning, but he allowed himself a short lie-in, and Alison was already at breakfast when he reached the kitchen. "Hello again," he said, kissing the top of her head. "Funny how when you're ill you can't remember what it feels like to be well, and vice versa."

Alison didn't answer. In her view the secret of a good, long-term relationship was never having breakfast together, except perhaps at weekends and holidays when there was no hurry. She had not shared this insight with Nick, who was under the impression that it was nice for them to have one of their rare breakfasts together.

"I've been thinking of taking up riding again," she remarked a few minutes later, spreading toast thickly with butter and marmalade. "I could get a pony."

"I didn't even know you rode."

"Not since Cambridge. It might be rather fun to take it up again. We've got the paddock just standing idle and there's that stable up on the moors. I could take some refresher lessons. It's silly to live in such perfect hacking country and not ride."

"It's not a bad idea," Nick agreed. Horses made him nervous, but if Alison was in one of her lady-of-the-manor moods, he wasn't going to argue.

"I'll go up there today and inquire," she said. "Want to come? You could take lessons too."

"No fear," he said. "You're not getting me near anything that bites at one end and kicks at the other. Hang on. Are you talking about the Colt's Head stables?"

"That's right. Why? You're not about to arrest everybody there and close them down, are you?"

"It doesn't matter." There was, come to think of it, no earthly reason why Alison should not use those particular stables. "Are there any eggs?" he asked.

"We're fresh out of eggs." Alison had spent the last week communing with some American bankers who wanted a software package written.

Nick poured himself a bowl of muesli. "Good job I've still got all my own teeth," he said, removing a particularly inpenetrable nut from the bowl.

"Momentarily," she said.

"You're rationed to one Americanism every ten minutes," he said. "If you exceed your quota, I shall sit on you until you scream."

"Sonofabitch."

"Nick!" Mike Brewster's voice boomed across the saloon bar of the Eagle and Child that lunchtime. "Over here."

Nick took his half pint of Golden Hill and sat down at the corner table with Mike—the police pathologist—and a large, shaggy-looking and moustached man, bearing a remarkable resemblance to an old-English sheepdog, whom he didn't recognize.

"You've had your hair cut," Mike said. "Reg been on at you about it?"

"He offered to do it himself with his pruning shears. I keep telling him if they wanted detectives to look like coppers they'd put us in uniform." Nick looked at the other man inquiringly.

"Oh sorry," Mike said. "This is David Hazlett-Jones, known to his friends as Davey Jones. He's the new consultant gynecologist at the hospital. Davey, this stripling is Detective Chief Inspector Nick Trevellyan, who is, believe it or not, head of Hopbridge CID."

Hazlett-Jones looked suitably impressed and the two men shook hands. "I see what they mean," he said, "about how you know you're getting on when the policemen start to look young."

"I know I'm getting on when the consultant gynecologists start to look young," Nick said gallantly. In fact, although Hazlett-Jones wasn't that much older than Nick—about forty—he carried his burden of years rather heavily, tending already to the *embonpoint* and the pompous suit.

"You should have heard my lecture yesterday, Nick," Brewster said. "I surpassed myself. I was superb. 'Some morbid conditions of the liver.'"

"With pictures of your own liver as illustration?"

"Get stuffed!"

Brewster laughed good-naturedly. He was a tall, thin man of about fifty, a grandfather twice over and one of the most stable people Nick knew. Nothing seemed to ruffle his easy temper, and he could carve up dead bodies with skill, precision and apparent unconcern for the smells and the stickiness that always accompanied them.

"He's gone," he had once explained to Nick as he stood gagging over a body—a suicide, as it turned out—four days

34

in the water. "Whatever there was in him that made him Bob Smith or Terry Jones moved on four days ago. This is just water, tissue, bone, hair, a handful of chemicals worth a few pence on the open market."

Over the last two years his hair had turned dramatically white with a speed which caused people to ask if he had perhaps seen a ghost. But Mike Brewster did not believe in ghosts. When he said the essence of Bob Smith or Terry Jones had moved on, he meant that it had dissolved into the ether and lived on only in the minds of those who had known him.

He lived well, ate and drank copiously, stated often that he knew, as a doctor, that these three score years and ten on earth were all he was going to get. He laughed a good deal at other people, but also at himself. He expected a lot from other people, but also from himself. His blunt humor could disconcert the uninitiated. There was nothing he wasn't capable of saying if it flashed into his mind to do so.

"Come here to meet a snout?" he asked Nick.

"If I had, I'd hardly be sitting here talking to you, would I? I've arranged to meet Alison here, as it happens. She's buying me lunch."

"I met your, um, girlfriend a couple of weeks ago," Hazlett-Jones volunteered. "At Lady Armitage's."

"Oh yes? You got inveigled into one of Molly's welcome-to-Hopbridge afternoons, did you?" Molly Armitage was Alison's godmother.

"Lady Armitage seems like a very nice little old lady," Hazlett-Jones said without much conviction.

Mike hooted with laughter. His laugh was very loud, and other people in the pub turned to stare; a few began to laugh themselves although they couldn't have said what at. "She's little and old and a lady at least," he said. "I'll pass on the first bit. I don't like *nice* people anyway. How is the lovely Alison, Nick? I haven't seen her lately."

"Very well as always. I don't think she's had a day's illness in her life."

"Pity," Mike said. "I wouldn't mind an excuse to examine her thoroughly. Magnificent specimen. Don't you think so, Davey? Lovely bone structure."

Hazlett-Jones went a little red before recovering well enough to say roguishly, with a good deal of moustache play, that bone structure was not his particular field of expertise in women. His remark put a thought into Nick's mind.

"Isn't it a bit awkward in your specialism, examining women you know socially?" he asked.

Davey shrugged. "It's all in a day's work."

"Bit like you having to interrogate people you know socially," Mike said.

"I always find that acutely embarrassing."

"We've all got parts of our bodies and minds that we don't want people sticking their cold fingers into—or their long arms in your case." Mike chuckled. "When are you two going to start a family, anyway? It's your civic duty. Good, healthy, stable, well-adjusted couple."

"You'd better ask her. I'm all for it."

"You just want to tie her down to you." This jibe was a little too near the bullseye for comfort, but Nick managed a thin smile. Hazlett-Jones looked very glum, too, and said quietly, "I had three kids but it didn't stop my wife taking off to live with an important surgeon with a house in Hampstead and a 'Sir' in front of his name."

Mike had the grace to blush. "Sorry," he said. "This hot weather has an odd effect on me. Incidents of sexual assault increase in the summer, you know. In fact you can find a positive correlation between sales of ice cream and reported rape"—he emptied his pint of beer with a lavish swig—"similar to that between alcohol consumption and cirrhosis of the liver."

"Is that true?" Hazlett-Jones asked Nick.

"I'm afraid so."

"Which proves," Mike went on, "according to some people's logic, that eating ice cream causes rape. Or vice versa."

"I suggest we change the subject," Nick said.

"I never even see them these days." Davey Jones was not to be deflected from his own sad story. "He's the one they call 'Daddy' now. 'Sir.'"

"Surely the court will give you access?" Nick said.

"It's not as simple as that. You have to think about what's in the children's best interest. I used to have them at weekends for a while, but then Diana—that's my wife . . . ex-wife—said it just unsettled them. She said it wasn't fair—"

"No, it certainly doesn't sound like it," Nick agreed.

"That's partly why I applied for the job down here," he sipped morosely at his beer, "to get away."

"Hello!" Mike said thankfully. "Talk of the devil."

Alison sat down next to Nick. She had already furnished herself with a large glass of something with ice and a slice of lemon in it. She was wearing an oversized blue and white T-shirt with a pair of skin-tight leggings, which she claimed were all the rage in London but which still made small boys in Hopbridge call after her in the street that she had forgotten to put her skirt on.

"Hello," she said. "I might have known I'd find the most important men in town here at this time of day. Hello, David. Nice to see you again." She gave him her sexiest smile and he basked in it and fidgeted some more with his moustache. She looked at Nick more closely. "You've had your hair cut." Her tone was accusing.

"Uh huh."

"They used the wrong size bowl."

"I had it done at the barbers in Sheep Street."

"Yes I can see you didn't go to a proper hairdresser."

Nick had to admit that they had taken off rather more than he had intended, but that meant he wouldn't have to get it done again for ages, and Reg would love it.

"Do you mean that squalid little place next to the butcher's?" Mike asked.

"Mmmm. I sometimes wonder about their meat pies."

"Sort of place where they ask you if you want anything for the weekend?"

"Mmmm."

"I don't see you as their sort of clientele. I had you marked down as what passes in Hopbridge for a Yuppy."

"They've got an interesting collection of magazines there," Nick told him.

"I'd have thought you were a bit young to be fitted for the dirty raincoat," Mike said.

Alison gave Nick an odd look: she knew he wasn't interested in that sort of thing. He had wanted to see what the legal end of the porn market was allowed to publish—as opposed to the sort of stuff that Bottone was peddling. It wasn't much better except that it featured grown women and not children. He had also wondered vaguely whether he might be offered something more spicy from under the counter if he betrayed an interest in the unappetizing crotch-shots on public display. Unfortunately he was a little too well known in Hopbridge for that to be likely.

He wasn't going to explain all, or indeed any, of this to

Mike and David: about these antiseptic pictures of women who were not whole, but just discrete parts—breasts and bottoms and vulvas and wide-spread mouths; about the joylessness of disconnected lust.

"To talk shop for a second," he said instead. "When are you going to do the PM on Bottone, Mike?"

"What's the hurry?" Mike asked. "Chap hanged himself. Since when are you interested in suicides?"

"I'm interested in all unexplained deaths."

"Only too easily explained, from what I hear. Why does anyone commit suicide, though? If you want to die, for heaven's sake, all you need is a little patience!"

"Just answer the question," Nick said.

"This afternoon. May I be allowed to finish my beer in peace first? Whatever they offer you by way of bribe or blackmail, Davey, do not consent to become a police pathologist. You can't call your life your own."

Hazlett-Jones murmured that they would hardly be likely to ask a gynecologist.

"What time are you doing it, though?" Nick persisted.

"Kickoff about two-thirty. Why? You in the market for a front-row seat? Cheap?"

"I'll be there." Nick drained his glass and got up. "Well, this is no company for a modest young girl," he said to Alison.

"Mayn't I be allowed to finish my gin and tonic in peace?" she asked, apparently recognizing the description.

"Not unless you want me to leave before the pudding. Hurry up, woman, I'm starving. I didn't get my breakfast egg."

"I remember when he used to talk to me with respect," she said, "when my smallest wish was his command. But that was three years ago and now it's 'hurry up, woman.'" But she tossed the rest of her gin down, gave Davey another of those smiles which had him molesting his long-suffering moustache again and followed Nick to the door.

"Don't eat anything too highly colored," Mike called after him. "It makes such a mess on the floor."

"I was only ever sick once," Nick said with dignity. "And even then I made it to the basin."

"So how did you get on at Colt's Head?" Nick asked when they were settled in the Pheasant's tiny garden and had placed their order. "Have you booked your first lesson?"

"Not exactly. I had a bit of a look round the place; it seems quite well run. They didn't take me in the stables, which is perhaps not surprising in the circumstances, but all the horses were out in the field anyway. There's a four-teen-hand bay gelding they start people off on until they see—"

"Sorry. A what?"

"A medium-sized brown horse, male but with its bits and bobs cut off," Alison translated. "It's middle aged and placid—just the thing for someone who hasn't been in the saddle for almost ten years."

"Did you meet the lady of the house?" Nick asked. "She interests me."

"No. There was no one about when I got there. I knocked at the house and a rather dim sort of stable girl opened it and asked if I was a reporter. When I managed to convince her I wasn't, she said the stables weren't open to-day, but I made out I'd come a long way and she agreed to give me a quick tour. She said they'd had a bit of family trouble and the owner was resting at the moment."

"A bit of family trouble. What a gift for understate-ment."

"She wasn't exactly chatty. Anyway, I said I'd think it over, then ring up and make a booking."

"And shall you?"

"I think so. I was remembering how good it feels to be up high on a horse's back on a sunny day on the moors, with the breeze in your face." She took off her sunglasses and threw her head back for a moment to demonstrate how good it might feel. Then she turned to the large tote bag she had been carrying with her and began to rummage in it, pulling a selection of carrier bags out.

"Been shopping?" Nick asked. "That makes a change."

"Well it occurred to me that I didn't have any of the right gear any more so I got some jodhpurs and riding boots— oh, and a new hard hat. Luckily the place in town had one to fit me. I have quite a big head, you know."

"No comment."

"And while I had my credit card out, I thought I might as well buy a new pair of shorts since there seems no sign of a break in the weather." She took out a pair of powder-blue shorts and shook them in the air to disperse the creases. "Washed silk."

"Very nice."

She frowned. "I suppose I'd better get my legs waxed if I'm going to go round flashing them at innocent by-standers."

It was strange, Nick reflected, how the feminine ideal of the late twentieth century—in the developed world, at least—was boyish: flat-chested, flat-buttocked, hairless— like a child, in other words.

6

Nick followed Mike Brewster back to his office when the postmortem was over. Mike stripped off his rubber gloves and threw them in the bin in the corner. He sat down and motioned Nick to do the same. Instead Nick stood looking out of the window. It had been cool in the air-conditioned postmortem room, and the weight of the heat astonished him afresh. He stared out at the brown grass and the thirsty earth.

"Mind if I get myself a drink of water?"

"Help yourself." Mike gestured at the sink in the corner. "Or I could manage something stronger." He tapped the top drawer of his desk. "Secret supply."

Nick shook his head. "Water will be fine."

"You look a bit green around the gills, but at least you kept your lunch today."

Nick let the tap run for a moment, poured himself a glass of water, drank it down in one gulp and refilled it. It didn't taste good but it was cold and wet. He splashed a little on his cheeks.

He was disconcerted afresh by how quickly a carcass went off, surrendering itself to bacterial life forms within hours of death, to maggots within days. He knew that it was part of Nature's endless recycling project, that a king must go a progress through the guts of a beggar, but it made you wonder what it was in the fragile breath of life that kept these horrors daily at bay.

Even then, it was not so much the uncomfortable fact of the corpse itself—the blood, the smell, the pale pink organs, the strangely quiescent heart, the competent slit of the surgeon's knife from gullet to groin—that upset him. It was the fact that Bottone, so alive, so involved in his own life, relaxed and boastful two days ago, was dead, his body cold, the top of his head sawn open, his innards severed and removed.

"I'm glad I don't have your job," he said.

"I'm quite glad I don't have any more PMs to do myself actually. Fortunately, we're not a homicidal lot in the Hop Valley."

"Don't you believe it." Nick sat down.

"Only two murders in the last few years," Brewster pointed out. "Aidan Hope and the little Carstairs girl."

"And the lawyer chappy," Nick reminded him.

"Oh, I'd forgotten about him."

"He wasn't a very memorable sort of person, I'm afraid."

"Well, this certainly wasn't homicide. I'm sorry, Nick, but the simple fact is that the man hanged himself."

"You've no doubt at all?"

"None. The signs of manual strangulation are different from those of hanging, as you know. He hadn't been strangled, there were no injuries, no blows to the head, no puncture marks."

"He could have been doped though, orally."

"I suppose so. We won't know that for a few days, not until the pathology lab have had a look at the tissue samples. Judging by the appearance of his liver, I'd say the only drug we'll find in him is the one which oils the wheels of all our lives: alcohol."

Nick sat for a while, sipping his second glass of water and thinking. Mike watched him in silence, then said, "What's your problem? You're not convinced, are you?"

"It was too convenient."

"The man faced a stiff prison sentence, perhaps with solitary for his own protection, since he was, in a sense, a sex offender. Then there's the disgust of his family, friends and neighbors. He opted out instead. Who's it convenient for?"

"His customers. It's illegal even to possess child pornography, not to mention, as you say, the opprobrium of decent people when you're exposed. There must have been a list of his customers somewhere, but my people have been over every inch of his house and stables without finding it."

"So he destroyed it as soon as he got the chance."

"He didn't get the chance, Mike. The place was searched from cellar to attic while he was still in custody. We had the damn floorboards up. Then the SOCOs even cleared all the straw out of the stables yesterday. Cruickshank kept moaning about being a housemaid for a load of horses."

"He would."

"The only conclusion I can reach is that someone knew of his arrest as soon as it happened. That someone knew where the list was kept, stole it, probably destroyed it. I can't help thinking that that same someone then killed him to stop him naming names."

"His wife would know who came to the house that morning, surely."

"Shirley saw her. No one came to the house, but it's a public riding stables; people are in and out of the yard all the time. The chances are he hid it there somewhere, where his wife wouldn't run across it by chance."

"It's young girls in and out mostly," Mike pointed out. "Thelwell children."

Nick smiled, remembering the cartoons of fat little girls on even fatter ponies.

"And their fathers, dropping them off in the car. It's in the middle of nowhere."

"I see. What you're saying is that he could have numbered respectable, married, middle-class, professional men among his customers."

"Almost certainly. Bank managers, teachers, lawyers . . ."

"Doctors?"

"Uh huh."

"Policemen?"

"I pray not; but it's possible."

"Who better placed to know that he was about to be arrested?"

"That thought had crossed my mind."

"Naturally. You're forgetting one thing, Nick. The fact remains that he hanged himself."

"Perhaps." Nick got up. "I'm going to have a word with the wife myself tomorrow. Shirley doesn't seem to have got through to her."

"And the old Trevellyan charm will score where the down-to-earth Miss Walpole failed."

"Let's hope so."

"Will Reg let you go on pretending this is a murder investigation?"

"I've still got to track down his customers and his sources. The magazines we seized come from abroad—the States and West Germany mainly—they're not my pigeon.

But someone is taking the still photographs. Someone round here.

"Why round here? Far more likely to be London. Or some peaceful, picturesque village in the Home Counties."

"Instinct."

"The policeman's nose? Can't argue with that."

"If Reg won't give me the time and resources, then I'll do it on my own."

"Well that seems to be that."

Nick was sitting in the superintendent's office an hour later, having reported the findings of the PM. Reg Grey was standing by the window, looking up at the sky with a frown. He lingered there, an upright figure with his hands clasped firmly behind his back like the Duke of Edinburgh. He was a tall man; his hair had thinned to the point where just an inch or two of closely clipped grey framed the bald dome like a tonsure. The hot summer had weathered his wrinkled skin like tanned hide. It struck Nick that he'd often seen Reg looking worried lately. Who knew what secret cares haunted the superintendent: the ever rising crime statistics, perhaps; the lack of manpower; or something more personal, like retirement in two or three years, pensions, the loneliness of the redundant divorcé? He did not seem inclined to speak further, so Nick prompted him.

"Sir?"

Reg turned back into the room and hovered behind his desk without actually sitting down. "No need to waste any more resources on it."

"I'd like to pursue my investigation a little further if you have no objection."

"Oh, but I have. It's the middle of the summer, Nick. The schools are breaking up. I've got more men off on holiday than at any other time of the year. I really can't spare the manpower."

"Which reminds me: You know that Carol Halsgrove and Paul Penruan are off on holiday from Sunday?" Reg nodded. "I could do with someone from uniform to tide me over, do a bit of leg work. If I could pick someone reasonably intelligent, and he shapes up, we might think about training him as a detective—"

Reg was already shaking his head. "You can have uniformed help on a temporary basis if it's really needed, as always, but there's no question of anyone extra being moved permanently to CID. You know how things are, Nick. HQ is always asking for cuts: less overtime, more productivity. You've used a lot of man hours on this case already, many of them on overtime, and to very little effect, it seems to me—one insurance broker with his life in tatters, one man driven to suicide. When all's said and done, it's just a few dirty pictures."

"With respect, sir. I don't think you know what we're dealing with here."

"I was in the Vice Squad for a couple of years, remember?"

"That was more than twenty years ago, sir, before the trade in kiddy porn really took off. You were dealing with magazines featuring adult men and women—pretty tame stuff, too, in those days."

"A lot of it was very nasty indeed," the superintendent said, vaguely offended. "Although I suppose it's true that child porn was still in its infancy then."

Which might, Nick thought, have been better expressed.

"You're missing the point," he said quite patiently. "Adult porn is very professional and usually simulated. Child pornography is largely amateur. Don't you see what that means?"

"That it's badly made?" Reg hazarded.

"That it's hard core! What those photographs depict is not someone pretending to have sex with another consenting adult just to titillate a few jaded palates. It's a permanent photographic record of children being abused—boys as well as girls."

"Oh!" Reg sat down in his chair with a bump.

"And not by strangers either: not by men in raincoats who lure them into their cars with a packet of sweeties; not by leering perverts in dark alleys—that's what people like to think. No: by their fathers, stepfathers, schoolteachers, youth club workers—people they trust."

7

Nick had a sense of *déjà vu* when he was summoned to the superintendent's office late the following morning. Nothing had moved, not even the dust, certainly not the papers in the in-tray. The Queen still gazed serenely out from her Annigoni portrait on the far wall, satisfied that these, her servants, were keeping her peace in her realm. Reg was standing staring out of the window, looking worried, just as he had been the day before. As Nick came in, he sighed heavily, turned away from the window, and waving Nick to a seat, sat down himself.

"I was over at HQ first thing for the regular meeting of senior officers. The ACC (Admin) is concerned about the image of the local force as it appears in the press."

Nick nodded. He had read all about it in *The Times.* It was not just their own force; police forces all over the country were worried about the deterioration in the public perception of their officers. It seemed to have reached its lowest point since Operation Countryman had carried out its large-scale purge of corruption some ten years earlier. It had begun once more to be taken for granted that policemen were rough, loutish and, frequently, dishonest; and while Chief Constables liked to talk of a few bad apples, the press preferred to call it the tip of the iceberg. Some forces were talking about employing PR men, making changes in their corporate identity. They could have been ICI. The Assistant Chief Constable (Admin) had taken to the whole idea like a schoolboy to fudge.

"So what's the solution?" he asked. "Get Colin Burcombe to start up a charm school?"

Reg let out the little snort which was his version of laughter. "Not exactly. He's suggesting a big public relations exercise involving the *Western Argus.*"

The *Argus*, Nick knew, was the biggest-selling paper in the West Country with a circulation fast approaching a quarter of a million. Its editor belonged to the same lodge at the ACC (Admin).

"And?" he said.

"And he would like some of our best officers to be followed around by a reporter for a few days. They call it 'shadowing.' He gets to see what police work is really like—not just the banner headlines—and that officers are human beings with strengths and failings, families and mortgages, emotions and a sense of humor."

"I have an idea where this is leading," Nick said, resignedly.

"Obviously the officers in question must be above reproach. I'm actually paying you a compliment, Nick, by asking you to do this. As you implied a moment ago, it's hardly a task for Colin Burcombe. I want this reporter to see that my detectives are educated, courteous and intelligent young men."

There was no need to lay it on with a trowel, Nick thought.

"And if you're really short of manpower," Reg went on, "then this chap can do a bit of legwork for you." He beamed. "So really it's killing two birds with one stone."

Terrific, Nick thought. Not only was he reduced to running CID with one sergeant for the next couple of weeks, he now had an untrained busybody foisted on him as well.

"Be grateful it isn't TV South West," Reg continued, "otherwise you'd be getting mobbed in the street by fans come Christmas."

"Who, when, where," Nick asked, "and, most importantly, for how long?"

Reg consulted a sheet of pink paper with the force crest in dark red on the top—another of the ACC (Admin)'s recent innovations—and its new Latin motto: *Video Meliora Proboque*—I see and approve the better course. (Nick knew, as the ACC (Admin) evidently didn't, how the quotation continued: *Deteriora Sequor*—I follow the worse.)

The superintendent picked up a pair of reading glasses from the desk, put them on and read out, "Mr. James Humbleby. You can expect him some time Monday morning. He'll call for you here, so if you could arrange to be in when he comes, that would get us off to a good start."

"And the most important question?"

"Um. A couple of weeks. Or so."

"You said a few days!" Nick objected.

"A few days, a couple of weeks. Let's not split hairs."

"I'm not sure about all this, Sir. How much am I supposed to show him? So much of our work is confidential."

"The buzzword at the moment is 'open policing'—justice being seen to be done. Only the most sensitive material is to be kept from him. Use your judgment."

"All right." Nick made a note. "James Humbleby. Ace Reporter." He also made a mental note to use not so much his judgment as sleight of hand.

"I'm relying on you, Nick," the superintendent said. "Be nice to him."

8

His telephone was ringing as he got back to his office. It was Sergeant Appleby, on duty at the front desk.

"There's a young lady asking for you, sir," he told Nick, "a Miss Fielding . . . and friend."

"I'll come down," Nick said. He scurried down the stairs and out into the reception area. A young black woman of head-turning loveliness was sitting on a bench, reading the "wanted" notices. A baby sat in its pushchair by her side, regarding the grubby, off-white walls with silent disdain.

"Lucy. How nice to see you."

She was an old girlfriend, from before the Alison era, and it was months, at least, since he had seen her.

She turned her face toward him and smiled, but he sensed that a lot of effort had gone into curving those wide pink lips into the required social gesture. She held out a hand to him silently, and he squeezed it and let it go.

"And who have we here?" He crouched down in front of the pushchair. The baby eyed him solemnly, not thinking much of him. "She's lovely."

"Well spotted," Lucy said. "Most people think she's a boy."

"It may be something to do with the blue Babygro," he pointed out. "What's her name?"

"*Hortense*," she said, pronouncing it in the French way. Nick groaned. "Sadist."

"It's a perfectly good name," she said. "It's very popular in Martinique."

"She's not living in Martinique. May I pick her up?"

"Sure." She leaned over to unfasten the strap, the beads in her braided hair jangling as her head moved. Nick picked the tiny girl up carefully, supporting her head as his sister had once taught him to do with his Australian nephews. The baby continued to look at him, unmoved and unsmiling.

"Not very chatty, is she?"

Lucy shook her head and her braids clattered together like a percussion section. "She just watches and thinks. When she really starts talking, I can't wait to hear what she's figured out."

The baby was a golden brown, much lighter than her mother. Her hair, though black as coal, was straight and fine, almost Orientally so. Her eyes were a deep liquid brown, and her pupils grew smaller as a shaft of sunlight passed across her face when the door opened, until the iris was fully visible. Then she closed them to shut out the glare.

"White father?" Nick asked.

"You know I only sleep with white men—positively racist, I am."

"Why is that, anyway?"

"They have bigger pricks."

Nick laughed. Sergeant Appleby glanced up briefly from his *Daily Mail,* looking puzzled, but Lucy did not so much as glance in his direction to see how her provocative remark had gone down.

"Well." She got up. She had had a Frenchwoman's knack

with her clothes, but today she looked carelessly thrown together in a full cotton skirt of unflattering mud colors and a yellow blouse which could have been cleaner. She wore rubber flip flops on her feet, and her toenails were overlong and ragged. He thought she was thinner than she had been.

"I'm just doing the rounds," she said, "showing everyone how clever I've been. We're going for a walk in the park now. Come on, sweetheart. Nice ducks. She likes the ducks." She took Hortense from Nick and secured her into her pushchair once more.

"Hold on." He glanced at his watch. "It's lunchtime. I'll come with you, if I may."

"Course you may. Hear that, Hortense? Uncle Nick is coming with us." The baby dribbled.

Nick held the door open and helped her down the steps of the police station with the pushchair. He wheeled it a few hundred yards along the pavement with Lucy padding silently at his side. Her step lightened as they walked, as if something of the summer warmth had entered her heart suddenly. "It's so nice to have someone helping," she explained, "in however small a way." They turned into Riverside Park.

"That bloke on the desk," Lucy said, "what d'you call him?"

"The duty sergeant. Dave Appleby."

"He was giving us funny looks."

"I expect it was that remark about white men," Nick said severely.

"I like to overturn racial stereotypes whenever I can, Bwana. No, he thinks she's yours."

"You reckon?" Nick shrugged. "I don't much care what Dave Appleby thinks."

"Good for you."

"Who is her father, as a matter of interest?"

"A young Parisian I met in Avignon."

"Ah. That explains her air of effortless superiority."

"Idiot! He was a student, about twenty."

"Cradle snatcher!"

"I didn't rape him. He was young, intelligent, good-looking and interested. I realized he was ideal. He need never even know that he'd fathered a child."

"Call me old-fashioned—"

"You're old-fashioned."

"But what happens when she starts asking who her father was?"

"I shall tell her the truth. After all, she's a very wanted baby."

They sat down on a bench by the pond. The fountains had been switched off in the last few days; South West Water had applied for a regional drought order. In the distance, beyond the more formal gardens, preparations were well underway for the annual summer fête and gymkhana. Men were building fences for horses to jump over; marquees were being erected, sawdust scattered. Nick did not envy them their activity. Hortense showed her first sign of animation as a duck waddled past.

"Dada!" she exclaimed, pointing.

They both giggled. "I'm glad, on the whole, that she didn't say that to *me* in front of Dave Appleby," Nick admitted. "What's happening about your work, Lucy?"

"Oh, I'm on indefinite leave from the comprehensive. I've bought a little cottage in the middle of nowhere, with roses round the door and a view of the sea. I'm going to be a full-time mother."

"I wish you both joy, and hope you won't be lonely."

"It wasn't a decision I took lightly, Nick."

"I'm not criticizing, Lucy."

"You, of all people, know that respectable middle-class marriage is not a guarantee that children will be loved and cared for. How many cases of child abuse have you come across over the years?"

"Not my job, thank God, I leave that to the uniformed branch and the social workers. . . . You're right, of course. Hortense could hardly have a better mother."

"Thanks."

"Apart from lumbering her with that name."

"No doubt you and Alison will call your children terribly boring, middle-class things like Henry and Edward and Elizabeth," she said tartly.

"I expect so," Nick agreed.

Lucy leaned back on the bench and let out a long sigh. "God, it's hot. Where do all these people," she waved her hands, "get their energy from?"

"All what people?" Nick teased her.

The only other people in sight at the moment were a young man of about twenty-five with a small girl clinging tightly to his hand. As Nick and Lucy watched, they stopped at the side of the pond and the father took a heap of stale bread out of a plastic carrier bag and gave a slice to the child, who tore it into pieces and began to throw it to the ducks.

A greedy swan came swimming over to them and lurched out onto the bank, its wings flapping alarmingly. The little girl screamed and went to run away but her father caught her up in his arms and swung her high in the air, away from the swan who was not so brave as he liked people to think and was already retreating at the noise.

"Daddy's here," he kept repeating in a sing song chant. "Daddy's here. Karen's safe. Nasty old swan won't get Karen—not while Daddy's here."

He kept swinging her back and forth until she stopped screaming and began to laugh with excitement. Then he lowered her gently to the ground and hugged her hard against him.

"Daddy! Daddy!" the child cried. "More swings."

He laughed. "Too hot," and gave her some more bread for the ducks. When all the bread was gone, the child demanded a ride on the slide and he took her hand again and led her towards the playground.

"Hello, Steve," Nick called out as they passed his bench.

The young man stopped and said, "Mr. Trevellyan," in a neutral tone, and blushed. He was a nondescript youth, neither very tall nor especially strong-looking. He wore his brown hair a little long and held it back with a headband like a tennis player, giving his face a cramped look. He had regular features with a weak mouth; his eyes darted all around: over Nick's shoulder, along the pathway, anywhere but straight ahead. His clothes were serviceable—blue jeans, white T-shirt with the name of a pop group printed on the front, dusty trainers without socks.

"How are you?" Nick asked.

"Well enough." He stood awkwardly, shifting from foot to foot, hanging his head. "Fine really."

"Not working?"

"Evenings, delivering stuff in a van, for Cronan's catalog. You know? The big mail-order company?" Nick nodded. "Lots of call for it now with so many people out at work all day. That way I can look after the littl'un during the day while Sheila's at work at the dairy."

"Your daughter?"

"Karen." He lifted his head now and stopped shuffling. "She's three." He seemed to grow taller as his back straightened and he looked Nick in the eye.

"I didn't know. Congratulations."

"Thanks."

"Well, don't let me keep you. Hope not to see you again—not in any official capacity, that is."

"No, sir." He looked down proudly at the child. "You won't." He picked the little girl up again, supporting her weight with a hand under her bottom, and pressed her to him as they moved off. "Who's Daddy's little sweetheart, then?"

"Bye, Karen," Nick called after them. "'Little lower than the angels,'" he murmured.

"Is he a thumping crook?" Lucy asked when he was out of earshot.

"No. Steve Clayton—vandalism, petty larceny. I like to think I nipped that one in the bud." He looked at his watch again. "I'd better be getting back. Where is this cottage of yours? Give me your address."

"High Wind Cottage. It's off the main road along the coast beyond Hopcliff. Pink-washed and thatched—"

"I know the one. Used to belong to an old couple called Gentleman."

"That's the one. I bought it from the Gentlemans, or should it be Gentlemen? Anyway, they were getting on a bit and going into sheltered housing near their daughter in Taunton."

"It's quite a big place. A good couple of acres of garden too."

"Babies need space."

"What I mean is, it must have cost a few bob." She

looked slightly embarrassed and didn't answer. "Luce? Come on, spill the beans. Don't tell me you diddled the Gentlemen—senile old couple, thought the place was still worth the seven hundred quid they paid for it in 1952?"

"Bloody cheek! Look, you remember my dad died a couple of years ago?"

"I remember. You were upset, very scratchy for ages and wouldn't tell me what the trouble was."

"Yeah, well. He left me everything, seeing as Mum and the boys didn't bother to come over from Martinique when I cabled them he was dying."

"Everything being what? I thought you were a child of the people, brought up on the outskirts of Wolverhampton without any shoes to walk to school in."

"Now, I never told you that."

"It was implied."

"He owned a string of little chemist shops all over the greater Birmingham area."

"Well, bugger me!"

"I sold them just before the bottom dropped out of the commercial property market."

"What a clever little capitalist it is."

"Do you want a thick ear?"

"And you didn't feel the urge to give all this money to the Socialist Worker's Party."

"No. My kid comes first. All right?"

"All right by me. Oh, Lucy, don't look so cross; you know I'm only teasing. I'm very pleased for you—pleased that you're able to bring up your baby in the way you want." He got up. "I really must go. But I'll come and visit you."

"Promise?"

"I promise."

■   ■   ■

They said that one child in ten was abused, whoever They were. There were other Theys who said the proportion was secretly much higher.

Guardians of the law, such as himself, and of society—doctors, nurses, social workers—were urged to be on their guard continually for the signs even though, or so it seemed to Nick from his limited experience, all children were fascinated by bums and willies, made up rude versions of nursery rhymes, were occasionally lazy or listless or lost their appetites for no obvious reason.

Was his refusal to believe the statistics just head-burying? He thought of all the families he knew or had known over the years. There was Bill Deacon, his regular sergeant, and his wife, Susie, with their three teenage daughters, all so different: Sarah, quite the young woman now at seventeen; Chrissie, at fourteen, scholarly, self-contained, grave; Trudi, a boisterous twelve and still mad about horses.

Then there was his sister Gwen, far away on the other side of the world, passing on the loving, hugging family life they had both enjoyed to the next generation in the form of his two tousled, athletic nephews. Doug, his macho Aussie brother-in-law, would sooner die than let any harm come to those two boys, let alone assault them himself.

And look at Steve Clayton, the young man in the park that afternoon. He'd gone from being a teenage tearaway to a family man. He was obviously devoted to that little blonde girl in her pink cotton frock and frilly knickers and pigtails, protecting her from swans and sick men with cameras. It would be a pity if fathers became afraid to pick up their daughters, to enjoy bathtime with them, to hug them, for fear of unnatural lusts.

Home: it was the place you went to be safe, to escape from the hazards of the world outside. Your parents: they were the people who protected you from predatory strangers, kept you warm, fed, loved. When home became the seat of danger, it was as though air had become unbreathable, water undrinkable. Where, then, could you turn?

9

The woman who answered the door of Colt's Head House
at two o'clock on Saturday was unmistakably its mistress,
brazen in her authority. She was in early middle age—
perhaps forty-five; a short woman and slightly built, her
presence filled the doorway. She wore jodhpurs with an
open-necked blue polo shirt and black riding boots. Shoul-
der-length blonde hair was caught back in a black velvet
Alice band. High cheekbones emphasized a skin without
blemish or artifice. Her grey eyes examined Nick, and the
corners of her broad mouth lifted almost imperceptibly in
a smile of inquiry.

"Mrs. Bottone?"

"Yes. That's me." Her voice was low in pitch: classless,
regionless, the tone neutral.

"I'm a police officer. May I come in?"

Her left hand moved awkwardly to her throat, which was
long and white but a little creped—the best indication that
she was no longer quite young and the first sign she had
given of anything other than the utmost composure.

"May I see your identification?" Nick showed her his
warrant card and she read it with care. "I've had the press
round, you see."

"I quite understand." While she examined the card, he took a mental step back to get the whole picture—the wood as well as the trees. She was still attractive in a clean, wholesome way. He could see how her unruffled looks might have appealed to a hot-blooded younger man like Bottone.

The hand she held out to him was as small as a child's, ringless, cool, but her grip was strong enough to control the most frightened horse.

"I don't mind for myself," she said, "but they pester the girls. We're in the back. You won't mind?"

She turned away without waiting for an answer, and Nick followed her through a wide hall, more like an extra room than a mere entrance, where silver cups and trophies filled every available surface space and red and blue rosettes covered the walls. Copies of *Horse and Hound* and *Country Life* lay heaped on a glass-topped table in the center.

"Do you ride?" she called over her shoulder.

"Er, no."

"Pity." She strode ahead of him, not looking round, assuming he was following. He thought of how Colin and, later, Shirley had spoken of her: aloof, yes; stuck-up, that remained to be seen.

The room she led him to—part kitchen, part family room—took up the whole of the back of the house. It was filled with pets, herbs, cushions, flowers, pictures, sunlight; shelves of books lined every alcove. The back door stood open into the stable yard. It was one of those doors where the top and bottom half open separately, which are known, aptly in the circumstances, as stable doors.

"We mostly live in here," Mrs. Bottone said, turning back to face him at last.

At the table four pretty little girls, ranging in age from about two to about ten, were tucking into a dish of cannelloni and a bowl of salad. Each one had long blonde hair, neatly pig- or pony-tailed, and huge gray eyes. All except the youngest wore riding clothes. Each of them carried on eating while staring at Nick in a way which would have unnerved a lesser man.

"We're running a little late today," she explained. "Still at lunch."

"My name's Nick Trevellyan," he said. "From Hopbridge police station. Sorry to disturb you."

"Laura Bottone. We've nearly finished. Would you like some cannelloni?"

"Er, no thanks. I've eaten. It smells lovely."

"These are my daughters: Feckless, Graceless, Aimless and Pointless."

Nick laughed and looked again round the welcoming room. "This place doesn't look much like Cold Comfort Farm to me. What are their real names?"

"I'm Felicity," said the largest girl, who sat at the head of the table, nearest to him. "I'm nine. How do you do." She turned her child's candid smile on him briefly before helping herself to some more tomatoes.

"Er, how do you do." Nick said, startled.

"I'm Grace," said a slightly smaller one. "I'm seven. How nice to meet you." She stretched across for a jug of orange juice and refilled her glass.

"I'm Amy," the third child piped up. "I'm four and a bit. Hello." She banged her spoon against her plate and got a warning look from her mother. Nick looked inquiringly at the youngest, who didn't seem old enough to be talking properly, but he was no longer prepared to take anything for granted.

"The baby is Patience," Felicity said, "she's two and a quarter." Then she and the other two girls chorused: "And if ever a child was more inappropriately named—"

"Wanna get down," Patience yelled, in support of her sisters' assertion.

"Yes, just this once," her mother said, "so the Chief Inspector will have somewhere to sit. You've come about Arturo, of course."

Nick took the place on the wooden bench vacated by Patience, who had by now tottered out into the stable yard. There was something warm and furry purring at his feet, but he didn't like to look in case it turned out to be a lion.

"Have some zabaglione if you won't have anything else," Laura said. He hesitated. She smiled a full-blooded smile at him. "I see I've found your weak spot."

"I am rather fond of zabaglione," he admitted. "Yes please."

She looked at him critically. "Anyway, you're too thin. Doesn't your wife feed you?"

"I'm not married," he said accurately if misleadingly.

"No? Hmm."

She ladled out a great bowl of the lightest, frothiest, creamiest pudding Nick had ever seen. He ate it, aware of the unflinching gaze of the remaining three girls on him. He felt like some ancient king of Spain, doomed for life to eat his meals under the formal scrutiny of the whole court.

"Nectar of the gods," he said, when he had regretfully finished the last spoonful.

"He's a smooth talker," Felicity said. "But I think he's all right."

"I rather like him," Grace said.

"Nice shirt," Amy said.

Nick suddenly remembered why he had come and that

this was supposed to be a house of mourning. These females had penetrated all his usual defenses in minutes. He composed his features into a funeral-director's smile as he accepted a cup of coffee from Laura.

"It's all right," she said. "Arturo wasn't often here these last couple of years so we don't much miss him. Now I've shocked you." What was really shocking him was the way she read his mind with such apparent ease.

"Mrs. Bottone—"

"Why don't you call me Laura?"

"Laura," he conceded, feeling unequal to formality after eating her zabaglione. "I'd like to check a few points with you, if I may. I know you've already made a statement to my sergeant but—"

"Don't worry. I've been waiting for the organ grinder to show up. Feckless, Graceless, Aimless! Go and play in the yard." Grace and Amy jumped up obediently and ran out of the door. Felicity lingered but her mother disposed of her with a commanding toss of the head.

"Go and do something about Brimstone's mane; it's a disgrace. You're not riding him in the gymkhana until it's been pulled and shampooed—fine advertisement he'd be for the stables looking like that." Felicity frowned, picked up a metal wide-toothed comb from the sideboard, and followed her sisters reluctantly into the stable yard.

"She likes to know what's going on," Laura said. "She's old for her years." She sat down opposite him. "I'm afraid I may have been a bit brusque with your young sergeant. She pitied me, you see, and that's the one thing I can't bear. I will talk to you so long as you promise not to treat me as a grieving widow. I assure you I shall not be behaving like one."

"I promise."

"I do not believe in self-pity, only in remedial action."

The purring mass at his feet emerged, yawning. It turned out to be a hefty ginger tom cat—not so very unlike the lion of his imagining except in miniature. It ate some food from a bowl by the back door, did a series of complicated stretching exercises, then followed the children out.

"I wouldn't have thought you'd have got much pity from Inspector Burcombe," he said.

"The one who came to search the place the day you arrested Arturo? What a creepy man. He went off with my address book even though I said he couldn't; and you should have heard some of the questions he asked me."

"It's not his place to ask questions," Nick said sharply. "He's not CID; he's uniformed branch."

"But he wasn't in uniform," Laura pointed out.

"Well, he was uniformed branch working in plain clothes."

"I see. I think."

"What did he ask you?"

"He wanted to know if Arturo and I had a normal sex life. I said if he could define normal, I would give him an answer. He sort of leered and said that normal was Saturday night with the lights out in the missionary position." Nick could not help but smile. "The thing was," Laura went on, "I couldn't make out whether he was serious or not."

"I'm afraid I don't know either. But, um, was it? Normal?"

"Arturo wasn't a child molester, if that's what you're asking. And if he had been he would certainly never have laid a finger on his own daughters."

"Sorry. I have to ask."

"That's what policemen always say: I don't want to ask this but it's my job."

"That's because it's the truth."

"We were more or less separated," she went on, "for about two years now although he used to appear from time to time—when he was broke, as a rule. He went away last autumn and I didn't see him again until he turned up here about three weeks ago, asking for a bed. I wasn't about to let him in the house, but I said he could put up in the stable loft for as long as he liked. After all, he is the girls' father and he loved them, in his way, very much."

"Can you tell me a little about him. You make, if I may say so, rather a strange couple." He remembered Bottone in the interrogation room: bumptious, mocking, defiant as a naughty schoolboy. He seemed the wrong mate for this self-contained woman.

"I know." She laughed softly. "It was all a mistake, I suppose, from the start. He was a good few years younger than me, as you no doubt realize. He was rather handsome in those days, sort of rugged, masculine. That appealed to me, at the time. And he was . . . well," her pale cheeks took on the faintest hint of pink "sexy. Later he grew coarse and took to drinking. Perhaps it was my fault for taking him away from his country and his people. Perhaps he was homesick, unhappy."

She was speaking to him now as if he were an old, confidential friend. "It never really worked, but we kept splitting up and drifting back again—enough to have four children together, anyway. But since I found out what he's been doing . . . of all the hateful things."

"He was a dealer," Nick pointed out, "a middle man, not a consumer, of child porn."

"But that makes it worse, Nick. Can't you see? If he'd

been a pedophile, I'd have been shocked, okay, but I'd have felt that what he really needed was help, psychiatric help. But he was like the drug pusher who's not himself an addict, exploiting the weakness of others for financial gain—for the great god Money."

"I hadn't thought of it that way, but of course you're right."

She waved her arms as if to encompass the house and pointed out of the back door. "He didn't need money. We have all this. I own it, true; everything's in my name. But he must have known I wouldn't have let him go short. If he needed more money, he had only to ask."

"It can seem shaming to a man, I suppose, to have to ask his wife for money."

"Especially an Italian? Tell me about it."

Nick had recently heard this expression during Alison's American phase. He had learned that it didn't mean she wanted him to tell her about it.

"There was nothing to stop him getting a job, come to that," she continued. "He was young, healthy, fit, spoke English fluently. There can be no excuse for what he did."

She led Nick out into the yard towards the stable. Felicity was hosing down a white pony which was standing patiently with his rein tied loosely to a ring in the wall. Laura stopped and fingered his mane.

"That's better. This is Brimstone; he's Feckless's own pony."

"Birthday present," Felicity added. "He's nine, just like me."

The pony turned his head to focus on Nick. His eyes were bold and lustrous; his ears were small and alert and pressed back against his head as he identified a stranger. His mouth made contact with Nick's shirtsleeve, and he inhaled deeply, rolling his upper lip back over his nostrils in an alarming way.

"It's okay," Laura said, seeing Nick's expression. "Don't be nervous. He's just tasting you to make sure you're a friend. Horses have a secondary nasal organ which they use to examine thoroughly a new taste or smell. He's a Welsh mountain pony: strong, hardy, lovely mouth, lots of spirit—too much for most nine-year-old girls."

"But not for me," Felicity commented.

"Very nice," Nick said inadequately. At least this horse had the merit of being fairly small. He rubbed the moist patch on his sleeve.

"She's going to make a champion horsewoman," Laura whispered. Felicity, overhearing, smirked.

Laura led him round the back of the pony, administering a slap on the haunches as she went. Nick moved quickly after her; he was sure he'd read somewhere that horses didn't like you walking right behind them and proved it by kicking you; but Brimstone stood placidly, taking his shower, as though carved from moorland chalk.

"This is the stable block," Laura said, opening the door, "and this is my pride and joy, Golden Wonder."

The horse raised his head as if recognizing his name and gave a little whinny. He was indeed a pale gold in color with a creamy, almost white, mane and tail. He was large and intelligent-looking with delicate features and a fine skin. Laura went across the cobbled floor to him and reached up to stroke his cheek and neck; she had to stand on tiptoe. The horse bent his head to help her, pressing against her shoulders, nuzzling down her back.

"He's magnificent," Nick said, impressed despite himself. Suddenly he could see some point in mastering this Pegasus; it would be like taming the elements.

"He gets lonely all on his own in here. Horses are gregarious creatures. They don't mind who they have for company—humans, donkeys, goats, cats—so long as they have someone. So they don't really like being stabled, but he's recovering from a leg injury and I thought it best to keep him in for a bit."

"What, um, sort is he?"

"He's a Palomino," she said, "and he's my own special horse. I don't let the clients ride him. I paid three thousand guineas for him."

"Guineas?"

"We're old-fashioned in the horse world."

"You mean someone actually sits down with a calculator and works out how much that is in pounds and pence?"

"Calculator?" she mocked him. "Didn't you do simple arithmetic at school?"

Nick thought hard; he didn't want to be seen using his fingers. "Three thousand, one hundred and fifty pounds," he said at last.

"*Bravo!*" She gave the word an Italian inflection. She took a small cube of brown stuff that looked for all the world like dried mud from her breeches pocket and held it out to the horse, who snaffled it up eagerly.

"And he's entire," she said and explained, seeing his puzzlement, "he's not been gelded." He remembered that that meant he still had all the bits and bobs.

She turned away. "You didn't come to see Goldie. Let's go upstairs." She went ahead of him, up a set of wooden steps through a trapdoor. "Your people took everything," she said, when Nick had emerged at her side, "all his personal things."

The large loft space was half full of bales of hay. The other half, dusty in the sunbeams from a cracked skylight, was living quarters. A floor had been laid there of bare boards, roughly nailed down, unpolished but swept, topped by a crocheted rug whose rainbow of colors spoke of leftovers from more ambitious knitting projects. A camp bed had been folded away, with one blanket and an uncased pillow piled neatly on top. A bamboo chest had two wide drawers with two narrow ones above; each drawer stood slightly open and clearly empty. A mirror on a swing frame stood on top of it. Laura picked it up.

"I might as well take that back to the house. Arturo won't be admiring himself in it again."

A single wooden chair, a stripped and neglected Windsor dining chair, stood under the skylight. "That was the one he used, to stand on. I shifted it back up here. Not sure I want that back in the house."

Nick looked at the desolate room; it was like a cubicle in a cheap boarding house where new tenants come and go daily and no one knows their real names. Bottone had been cleared away; it was as if he had never existed.

"Which was the beam?" Nick asked as they stood down on the cobbles once more, looking up.

She pointed. "And you have the lunge rein."

"Yes. You can, er," he cleared his throat, "have it back eventually."

"Thanks." She gave him a mocking smile. "But no thanks. I'll take my address book, though, as soon as it's convenient."

"Of course."

"Do I seem hard to you?" she asked unexpectedly.

"Not hard, no."

"I just want to get on with my life. Pick up the pieces, help the girls to forget."

"Do they understand what their father had done? To get arrested, I mean?"

"I think Feckless half understands. The others are too young. Thank goodness."

"Amen."

"Arturo is dead, for better or worse. Protecting the girls is what matters now."

10

When he shook hands with the Ace Reporter at about eleven-thirty on Monday morning, Nick had to revise some of his prejudices. This was not the shark-toothed monster in a seedy raincoat he had been expecting. Humbleby was a meek-looking man in fawn slacks, brown T-shirt and, despite the continuing heat, a camel-colored cardigan. He was short, rather plump, balding and could have been any age from twenty-eight to forty. He had a small moustache which was unable to make up its mind whether it wanted to be toothbrush or develop a fine pair of handlebars. He was blinking behind his spectacles and looked a little like a mole thrust without warning into sunlight.

"Jim Humbleby." He had to put down a large nylon bag to engage hands. "They call me Bumble Bee at the paper because they say I just bumble along." He favored Nick with a smile of great sweetness.

"Nick Trevellyan, head of CID. Let me, er, help you with that." He bent to pick up Humbleby's case, but the reporter gave a little cry of alarm.

"I'd rather you didn't, if you don't mind. My camera equipment, you know, rather fragile." He picked up the bag, slung it heavily over one shoulder and began to follow Nick up the two flights of stairs to his office.

"I thought you chaps always had photographers with you," Nick remarked.

Humbleby giggled. "On the nationals, maybe. Anyway photography is my hobby." He set his bag down carefully on a chair in the office and unzipped it. He took out a camera and trained it experimentally on various objects in the room, adjusting two or three of a large number of dials and knobs.

"Leica R-five," he said with pride. "It's got four different exposure modes and a fifty-millimeter lens."

"Really?" Nick said politely. It made about as much sense to him as all that horse talk.

"I've got other lenses, of course."

"Of course."

"Can I take a picture of you sitting at your desk?" Nick sat down. "Look sort of . . . pensive, like you're trying to solve a really tricky case." Nick obliged. He frowned hard, trying to recall exactly what he had eaten for dinner the previous evening. He held the pose a long time while Humbleby selected the right lens.

"Perfect!" The reporter snapped away. "Just the job."

"Where are you staying, Mr. Humbleby?"

"Jim, please."

"Jim."

"At the Old Railway Hotel. The bathroom adjoining my room is perfect—it's got no external windows, you see."

Nick intimated that this sounded like a disadvantage, but Humbleby replied, "Oh, no. I can set it up as a darkroom and develop as I go along. It's perfect."

"Well," Nick said, unsure where to start with this beige lap dog. "I'm new to all this."

"Oh, me, too. Fairly new to the business actually." He leaned forward and spoke confidentially. "I hate all that Fleet Street hackery. It's so unnecessary—distorting stories for the sake of headlines, sensationalism. I like to think of myself as a New Reporter. Tell the truth and shame the devil."

"Oh. Good. Well, I suppose the idea is for you to just follow me around, jotting things down."

"And taking pictures, of course."

"I'd prefer it if you always ask me first about that. Some of my . . . customers may not take too kindly to being photographed."

"Hope you don't talk too fast," Humbleby said. "I can't do shorthand." He took out a notebook and pencil and looked expectant.

"I spend a lot of time in this office, as it happens," Nick explained, "doing paperwork." He paused as the reporter wrote this laboriously down. "People think I'm chasing around in police cars with sirens wailing all the time—"

"How do you spell 'siren' again? Is it I or Y?"

"It's nearly midday," Nick said rather desperately. "Why don't we nip across to the Eagle and Child for a drink before we really get started?"

"I don't drink," Humbleby got up and hoisted his camera bag onto his shoulder once more, "but I'll join you in an orange juice."

He went on chattering as he followed Nick down the stairs. "I live in Exeter, myself," he said. "Right in the center of town. It's so different, isn't it? Being out in the country like this—in a small town where everyone knows everyone and everything—"

"If only I did," Nick said, "know everything that went on round here."

"People are . . . you know . . . more *real* in the country. Don't you think?"

To his surprise, Nick found himself warming to this diffident young man who seemed so ill-adapted to his calling and whose head was so full of stereotypes. After an orange juice and a shared packet of crisps, he heard his own voice inviting Humbleby over for dinner one evening during his stay. He wondered what Alison would have to say about that. Humbleby, however, was thrilled.

"Oh, yes! The home life. I want to show you as just an ordinary guy in a semi with a wife and a couple of kids."

"Um." Nick's life didn't fit that description at all. The only person he knew in the Job who did fit it was Bill Deacon, and he was still on sick leave. "I'm not actually married."

"Me neither," Humbleby said. "No one's ever asked me. Ha ha."

"Although I do live with someone. It's not exactly a semi, though. Well, you'll see. Shall we say Wednesday night?"

"That would be lovely." Humbleby spoke with great enthusiasm. "Thanks very much, Nick. It's exciting, isn't it, all this police work? I can't wait to get started."

"It can seem like that at first, I suppose."

"You will let me help, won't you?"

"Perhaps a little leg work," Nick said cautiously, "or anything clerical." After all, his spelling couldn't be worse than Penruan's.

"Naturally I don't expect to be treated like a fully fledged detective, conducting skillful interrogations and wrestling villains to the ground and so on—"

"It really isn't much like that. Not as a rule."

"Just like *The Bill*. And how long have you been doing it?"

"Me? Fourteen years in the police, eleven in CID."

Humbleby scribbled away. "Tell me, Nick. My readers would love to know. Do you get depressed by the ever rising tide of crime at this moment in time, by the escalating violence of our society in this day and age, by feelings of helplessness in the face of evil?"

"Not really," Nick lied.

The tears which had never come to Lucy at moments of crisis flowed easily now and for no reason. It was as if the baby were stubborn—not wanting to come to eat when her breasts were heavy and sore with milk, not wanting to sleep when required. It was as if she did it on purpose.

She was sleeping now and Lucy sat in the armchair in her sitting room not doing anything, not looking at anything, leaving the tears to dry on her cheeks at will. The room was untidy where she could not be bothered to pick up a newspaper from the floor, could not be bothered to *read* a newspaper. There was a feeling of flatness to everything, as if the bottle of life had been left open too long and all the fizz had gone out of it.

On Friday, when she had walked to the park and back with Nick, with him pushing the buggy and negotiating steps and pavements, she had had a taste of what it might be like to share this burden. It was not that you wanted someone to make decisions for you, just to be there while you made them, to give moral support, to convince you that it didn't matter so much if you got it wrong. She felt so often anxious— she who had always been so calm. Hortense frightened her in her baby helplessness: when she was crying there seemed no remedy; when she was quiet it might be that she'd succumbed to sudden infant death syndrome.

The house was silent. It was the middle of the afternoon on a weekday; everyone she knew was at work. There was no one she could ring up and ask over for a coffee and a natter and an exchange of baby stories. She couldn't go out until Hortense woke up, and then she couldn't go out until she had changed her and fed her and burped her and dressed her and put her in her special seat in the back of the car and collapsed the buggy and put it in the boot and it was all just too much trouble. It was so much easier to stay here.

The car. Sometimes she imagined herself backing it into the garage, closing the door, running the hose from the exhaust through a crack in the window; making herself as comfortable as possible in the cramped back, with or without Hortense—the fantasy varied; switching on the engine with a full tank of petrol, waiting, knowing that soon she, they, would never have to worry about anything again. One of the things which stopped her was not knowing who would find them, and how, and after how long.

She didn't want to read, or to listen to *Woman's Hour* with its bright discussions on politics and feminism. There was a theory that nature prepared women for the long boredom of motherhood by numbing their brains with a carefully measured trickle of the right hormones. How else could you tolerate years of nappies and baby talk? She had felt almost bovine during pregnancy; she had been well— hardly any sickness, no varicose veins. Were the hormones beginning to wear off now? Was she being eased back into reality?

She closed her eyes. The tiredness was not physical; despite the midnight feeds, she could catch up on her sleep during the day. It was in her mind, all in her mind. Sometimes the room began to dissolve around her; she felt detached from the world as if living in a bubble.

There was someone she knew who might be around in the middle of the day—the woman who had been an unexpected comfort when her father died and she had felt so drained by it all. She picked up the telephone and dialed: Great Hopford 3462. It rang four times before answering. After a slight whirring, Alison's voice said, "Hello, this is Hope Cottage. I'm afraid there's no one here to answer your call right now—"

Lucy hung up. Upstairs a thin wailing began. Hortense was awake already; it could not be half an hour since she had settled to her sleep. She sighed and heaved herself to her feet muttering, *"Vous l'avez voulu, Georges Dandin. Vous l'avez voulu."* She grappled with the stairs.

As she reached the top, she heard a car pull up on the gravel driveway. She went into her own room, which faced the front, and drew the curtain aside to peer out. She had never seen that white BMW before, she was sure of it. It didn't belong to anyone she knew.

The driver's door opened and a young man got out—a very handsome young man. He must be lost. This road didn't lead anywhere except to High Wind. Such a very handsome young man: tall and fair and just the way she liked them—just the way she had once liked them, she corrected herself.

He reached across to the passenger seat and pulled out a camera case. She took a step back from the window as he looked up at the cottage, shading his eyes against the sun. She walked over to the mirror and began to fiddle with her hair. What a sight she looked. She was too thin. Her breasts ached. Her hair needed washing. Her face wasn't even clean. What were those stains down her cheeks? Tears? Of course.

Hortense had stopped crying as if by magic and gone quietly back to sleep. Even the banging on the front door did not waken her now. Lucy slipped into the bathroom and quickly bathed her face and tidied herself before going to see what all the fuss was about.

11

Nick was knocking at the door of a semidetached house in Dove Crescent at about the same time that afternoon. It was a prosperous-looking house with fresh paintwork and a tidy, well-stocked front garden, but he saw that all the curtains were drawn across, giving a secretive appearance to the place on this cloudless day. Four pints of milk stood on the doorstep, already yellowed and cheesy in appearance.

There was no reply to his knock.

"Nobody at home," Humbleby said. "Gone away by the look of it." He pointed at the milk bottles, proud of this minor piece of detective work, which he thought was not bad for a beginner.

Nick was not so sure. He stepped back a pace, looked up at the first floor, and saw a curtain twitch in the oriel window over the porch. He knocked again. Then he pushed open the letter box and peered through it. There were no lights on, and he could make out only the static shapes of a hall stand and a semicircular table with a potted plant drooping on it.

"Mrs. Tyson," he called through the slit. "Can you open the door please. I'm a police officer."

After two or three minutes he heard the sound of someone coming slowly down the stairs. Then she opened the door a crack, recognized Nick, and opened it an inch or two farther to say: "He's not living here."

"Can you tell me where I can find him?" Nick asked. "I've got a few questions I'd like to ask him."

Two young women with toddlers in pushchairs came along the street. They slowed down as they passed number eight, then stopped and stared openly, insolently. One of them whispered something to the other. Humbleby, to Nick's surprise, took out his camera and pointed it in their direction, feigning preparations for a shot. They moved on as rapidly as could be reconciled with dignity. Humbleby gave a little laugh.

"That'll teach them to respect people's privacy."

Nick looked at him with approval. "Nice one, Jim."

Mrs. Tyson flung the door open. "You'd better come in before the next lot of spectators arrive."

They followed her into the airless gloom of the hall. Nick endeavored to introduce Jim as a colleague, but she was not interested. A week had passed since her husband's arrest had brought her life collapsing in upon itself, and the transformation had been dramatic. A week ago—before she had been brought to the police station to confront her husband with that shaming charge—she had been an unremarkable housewife, coping well with the minutiae of daily life: the busyness of three young children and a home to run; the tight schedule of school runs and Brownies and the weekly shop and managing a budget.

She was a wispy, slightly faded woman of about thirty-five. Before, she had been neatly dressed, tidily turned out; now she looked exhausted. Her sandy hair was unbrushed, her face freckled and grubby with tears. She was in her dressing gown, although it was almost three o'clock in the afternoon; her feet were bare on the polished parquet. She smelled of neglect.

The house was silent: no radio played, no clock ticked, no pipe gurgled; it might have been dead.

"I've sent the children to my mother's," she explained, "to get them away from here." She looked round in helpless despair. Nick and Jim exchanged glances of sympathy.

"Why don't you sit down and let me make you some tea?" Nick said. "Or something cold might be better, some orange squash." He laid a hand on her hot arm and guided her gently but firmly along the corridor to the back of the house.

She went obediently into the kitchen and sat down at the table. Humbleby perched on the windowsill, out of her line of sight, and took out his notebook. Nick busied himself opening cupboards, looking for the things he needed. She offered no help. There was milk in the fridge, but it had a sour reek to it and he held out no hope for the bottles on the doorstep. He abandoned the idea of tea.

"Have you eaten today?" he asked. Or yesterday, come to that, or the day before.

"I've been getting things pushed through the door, you see," she said, not answering his question. "Letters . . . other things. Oh, yes, and phone calls. I've taken the phone off the hook." She pointed to a slimline telephone mounted on the kitchen wall, and Nick saw that it had, in fact, been not so much disengaged as wrenched from its socket. He glanced at Humbleby, who made a wry face.

"Have you reported all this?" Nick asked.

She looked at him as if she did not understand the question. "Last month, last *week,* I would have the done the same. I would have been the first to cast the stone."

"I'm sure that's not true." He finally found a bottle of lemon barley water and poured a little of the yellow syrup into three tall glasses.

"Yes, it is. If Mr. Carpenter," she gestured towards number six, the other half of the semi, "or Mr. Eubank," number ten, four feet and a wooden fence away, "had been arrested for what Wesley did, I'd have blamed him fast enough, blamed her. . . . Made their lives hell. . . . Not fit to live next door to decent people. . . . Well, we're not."

"You really mustn't blame yourself." Nick seemed to have spent so much of his life saying those five words to people, but what other way was there of putting it? He ran the tap until the water spurted cold into the sink, then mixed the lemon barley, handed Jim his, and joined her at the table.

"Why not?" she said. "Obviously I didn't meet his needs in . . . that department. I should have tried harder, done what he wanted more."

"It's not quite as simple as that, Mrs. Tyson," Nick said. "Look, have you another name?"

"Deborah."

"Deborah. Is it all right if I call you that?" She nodded. "Your husband is . . . ill. He needs help to stop him being a menace to himself and other people."

She was not listening. "Mrs. Eubank emptied her rubbish over the fence, into my garden. She said we were rubbish and that if she ever found out that Wesley had laid a finger on either of her boys, her Maurice would kill him." She looked pleadingly at him. "He never touched the children. I swear. He never. He'd never lay a finger on his own kids."

"I know that." The social workers had been to see the

Tysons. Wesley Tyson seemed to have confined his urges to fantasy. "When is the social worker coming next?" he asked.

"She isn't. Not now the kids have been sent away."

But she was in need of help, Nick thought, as well as her husband and children. He would have a word in the right quarters. It was a disgrace that she should have been left to fend for herself in this emotional state. Although emotional was not quite the word: what she seemed to be doing at the moment was suppressing all emotion.

"So, do you know where I can find Mr. Tyson?" he asked.

"He's living in some hostel, over at Hopcliff, for homeless men."

"I know the one."

"He's seeing the psychiatrist—the tall man at the hospital."

"Dr. Frobisher."

"He wouldn't go at first, said that he could see no point in getting help if I was going to divorce him anyway. So I said I'd take him back if he'd get therapy, sort himself out."

"That takes a lot of strength," Nick said. "I admire you."

She gave him that uncomprehending look again. "I haven't had a job in fifteen years, not since Tommy was born. Wesley looked after me, made the decisions—where we would live and what color we would paint the lounge and where we would go for our holidays and when. How would I cope if I left him? How would I live? Besides, I took him for better or worse, before God. We're chapel."

"Where will you go?"

"My family come from the Midlands, Leicester. We'll go there, start again where no one knows us. I'd put the house up for sale, but I can't abide the thought of all those Nosy

Parkers coming to view just to get a look at me." She murmured again, "Rubbish. That's what she said: rubbish." She rose suddenly. "You'll want to see where he kept it."

"Well, I—"

"This way. This way."

She left the room, and Nick and Jim followed her. They went upstairs into the smallest bedroom, the one over the porch. It was fitted out as an office with extensive filing cabinets, bookshelves, ring binders. An Amstrad computer and printer stood on the desk.

"He kept records on that," she said, pointing at the PC. "Intricate records, cross references, everything. He's always liked things to be neat and tidy. I used to tell him he was an obsessive, and he used to laugh and say 'You're not wrong, Mother.'

"I knew he had a program for cross-referencing his insurance sales. It was his favorite toy; he used to say that he could always keep ahead of the opposition because he could see at the touch of a button who had what insurance and just where there was a gap waiting to be filled.

"I never knew how it worked, never tried; he always said I wouldn't understand technical things, not a dunce like me. Then, yesterday, I took down the manual, see—", she picked up a handbook that must have been a thousand pages thick, "and just worked my way through it until I'd seen everything he'd got on there." She looked proud. "It took me nine and a half hours. Half the night."

"And what is there?" Nick asked, transfixed.

"Records of all the magazines and videos he'd bought. And there was an index, you know? You type in 'sodomy' or 'fellatio' and it'll tell you where to find the pictures, a brief description, whereabouts in the attic the magazine was stored."

It was clear that Deborah Tyson had never used those words before, was not entirely clear how to pronounce them or what they meant.

"Blimey!" Humbleby said.

"Child porn collectors are often obsessives," Nick told him. "God knows why."

"It's all gone now," she finished, and the two men followed her eyes to the trapdoor in the ceiling. "They took it all away. Your people."

"You wouldn't want all that stuff in the house with you," Nick said gently.

"I might have learned from it. Might have found out what it was he wanted that I wasn't giving him." She sat down in the swivel chair in front of the computer and began to cry.

Nick was at a loss. He couldn't leave her like this; she might do anything.

"Have you seen your GP?" he asked.

She shook her head. "I haven't been out of the house. I shall never be able to look anyone in this town in the face again."

"Have you got his number handy? I'll get him to look in on you while he's on his rounds this afternoon. Then you won't have to go and sit in the waiting room with other people." She didn't answer. "Who is your GP, Deborah?"

"Dr Savage."

"Fine. I know the number of the Health Center. I'll call for you." There was another telephone in the office and he saw that it was still connected although the bell had been switched off. As he went to lift the handset, the red light on the instrument began to flash. He raised it to his ear without saying anything, and a man's voice spoke in a low, monotonous whine.

"Fucking perverts. It's your children next. Don't think sending them away to Leicester will do any good—"

"I'm a police officer," Nick said, "and this call is being traced." The receiver was slammed down at the other end. He was glad that Mrs. Tyson didn't seem to have heard his words. Her home was no longer a place of safety either. He got through to the Health Center and spoke to Dr. Savage in person. Savage agreed to come round before evening surgery at about four o'clock.

Nick stayed with her until then. He sent Humbleby out for some milk and bread, some ham and cheese and fruit, which he paid for himself. He drew the curtains, opened some windows, and let the stale air out. He poured away the reeking milk and washed the bottles and put them back on the doorstep. He watered the potted plants. He persuaded her to take a shower and put a fresh dress on. While she was in the bathroom, Humbleby returned with the provisions, and they made her some sandwiches.

"I feel sorry for the woman," the reporter whispered as he spread butter too thickly, "but it's hard to believe she didn't know."

"Remember what they say about affairs," Nick reminded him, "the wife is always the last to know."

"I didn't realize policing included all this sort of thing." He waved his hand vaguely. "Almost like social work."

"That's part of what you're here to find out."

"Who was that on the phone just now?"

"A sick man with nothing better to do all day. Can't these people see that she's as much a victim as any of those poor kids?"

"Was it really being traced?"

"Of course not. That would have to be done from the exchange and I'd have had to keep him talking for several minutes while they did it. But he wasn't likely to know that."

"There's so much to learn. Er—"

"Yes?"

"Is that really how you pronounce 'fellatio'?"

"No."

She came down shortly after, all damp and shiny, ate as instructed, wept into her plate, spoke no more.

"So by the time I'd hung around to explain the situation to Ned Savage, gone out to get her prescription for antidepressants made up, rung up the social services and got a promise that a social worker would visit her tomorrow, got the beat constable to keep a special eye on her house and bullied British Telecom into putting an intercept on all her incoming calls, I thought I'd better call it a day," Nick said that evening.

"Sounds like you've had an eventful time," Alison remarked.

"Strange how differently people cope with disaster: there's Laura Bottone just quietly getting on with her life, and there's Deborah Tyson all set to have a complete breakdown."

"Here." She handed him a glass of Chablis. "For services above and beyond the call of duty."

"Thanks. I think I need this."

"Dinner won't be long."

"That reminds me." He told her about his impulsive invitation to Jim Humbleby. He knew that she was not overfond of reporters; they had given her a hard time when she had herself been a suspect in a murder case three years earlier. "He's quite nice really," he apologized. "Not like your common or garden reporter at all. Calls himself a New Reporter."

"Ah well," she said, "worse things happen at sea. Thinking about this nuisance caller of Mrs. Tyson's: you don't suppose Bottone could have been killed by someone like that out of revenge, do you, someone who feels very strongly about child abuse?"

"Rather than by a client? I suppose it's possible. There don't seem to be enough hours in the day at the moment to follow all the possible paths."

"And you really must go and see Lucy," she reminded him, since Nick had, of course, told her all about his meeting with his old flame and the promise he had made. "I'm not sure she realizes quite what a change the baby's going to make in her life."

"There are so many single-parent families nowadays," Nick said with a sigh, his mind still very much occupied with the subject of abused children. "Pedophiles have even been known to marry single mothers, you know, just to get access to their children." He shuddered. "Let's change the subject, for God's sake."

She immediately obliged. "I had my first riding lesson this afternoon on a placid old nag called Benjie. I wasn't as rusty as I'd feared and I managed not to fall off. I suppose it's like swimming or riding a bike: once learned, never forgotten. I did a bit of cantering, no galloping or jumping yet. I'm not sure Benjie *could* gallop even if the knackers' men were after him. I bet I shall have a few aching muscles tomorrow though—"

"The trouble with this sort of pornography," Nick burst out, "is that it gives a . . . what? . . . a *validation* to the pedophile."

She looked at him with affection. His inability to come

91

home and forget, put it all behind him, was one of the things that made him good at his job; but it could be a big strain on him at times, especially when it was something he felt passionately about. Her attempt to change the subject as requested had lasted less than two minutes.

"Darling," she said, "don't you think—"

"It shows him that his unnatural desires are shared by others," Nick was saying, "and that they're therefore perhaps not so very unnatural after all. Then he shows the magazines or the pictures to the kid he's abusing: 'Look, what we're doing is perfectly normal,' he says, 'but it's our little secret and you must be sure not to tell anyone.'"

"Children love secrets," Alison agreed, "especially ones shared with adults whom they admire and trust. For as long as I can remember, Dad used to take me to help choose Mum's birthday present, then swear me to secrecy. I used to hug myself for days, half wishing her birthday would hurry up so I could see her pleasure when she opened the parcel, half hoping the day would never come so I could keep this precious secret for Dad."

"And it may not even seem unnatural to the abuser. So many of them were abused themselves as children that it's the only way they know of relating to a child."

Alison gave up. "Come into the kitchen with me," she instructed. "Bring your drink. You can keep on talking while I'm mashing the potatoes."

12

"Are you going to be in tonight?" Alison asked Nick as he prepared to leave for the office the next morning.

"I think I shall have to go up to the stables again after work, on the pretext of returning Mrs. Bottone's address book. Why?"

"It's just that I ran into Davey Jones in town yesterday."

Nick looked blank for a moment, then remembered. "Oh, the tame gynecologist?"

"Yes he looked so lost and lugubrious that I invited him out to the pictures this evening. We thought we'd go and see *Woman on the Edge of a Nervous Breakdown.*"

"Well, don't take Mrs. Tyson with you."

"Are you taking your tame reporter to Colt's Head?" she asked.

"No fear. I don't want him writing about them, they have enough to put up with. That's another reason I shan't be going until this evening, when Jim's safely back in his hotel room."

"You keep talking about someone hanging him," Shirley said in his office an hour later, "but surely he'd have been bruised if he'd been manhandled onto the chair—that would have shown up at the PM. I don't believe it was physically possible. He wasn't an especially small man. Just imagine it for a minute."

"I thought I was being accused of having too much imagination," Nick objected.

"Jim." Humbleby looked up expectantly. He seemed to have taken a fancy to Shirley and was eager to please. "Be a drunken child pornographer for a minute. You're about the right size and shape."

"Anything to oblige a lady." Jim seemed unoffended. He stood up. "Where do you want me?"

"You agree, Nick, that if someone hanged Bottone, he must have been more or less unconscious at the time?"

"I'm prepared to accept that as a given. Everyone agrees that he'd been drinking, and he'd hardly have let them do it without kicking up a fuss otherwise. I mean, would you?"

"Right. Can you go limp, Jim?" Humbleby flopped like a puppet whose strings had just been cut. "Take up the slack, Nick." Nick put his hands under the reporter's armpits and heaved. The dead weight dragged on his arms. Humbleby, throwing himself into his part, began to sing a slurred drinking song.

"You can only just hold him up," Shirley pointed out. "Now imagine trying to heave him onto a chair, get the rope round his neck, keeping him upright—" Nick tried to pull Humbleby to his feet, but the plump man's legs splayed out in any direction but groundwards.

"'If I were the marrying kind, which thank the lord I'm not, sir,'" he warbled. "'The kind of man that I would choose would be a rugby full back. He'd push hard. I'd—'"

"Yes, thank you, Jim," Shirley said. "You've got the part. You can stand up now."

Humbleby's sandaled and besocked feet were immediately grounded, and he stood up and took a bow. "I had no idea police work involved so much variety and required so much raw talent."

"You see?" Shirley said to Nick.

"I see that it couldn't be done by one person working alone," he admitted.

"Satisfied now?"

"No."

A fairy, Nick thought from a distance. A fairy flying on a magic horse.

The horse, he saw as he got out of his car and strolled over to the paddock, was the stallion Golden Wonder. The fairy he had never seen before; he would have remembered. Hadn't Laura said that no one but herself rode Golden Wonder? He stood leaning on the fence, watching, as the fairy, oblivious of his presence, guided the horse over a series of jumps which looked dangerously high to Nick's untutored eye. If Goldie had been having trouble with his legs, he was fully recovered now.

He caught his breath in alarm as the horse rounded a corner, approached the next fence awkwardly, hesitated, changed legs at the last minute. He almost called out a warning, but the fairy squeezed the horse's ribs extra hard, leaned forward into his mane with her bottom high in the air, called out something that sounded like "Gerron!" and they cleared the fence together with six inches to spare.

Nick, finding that he had been holding his breath, let it out in a gust. The fairy brought the horse to a halt, patted his neck and walked him slowly back in Nick's direction.

"Hello there!" he called out.

She made no reply, sat there high above him, looking down at him. She was very young, he saw, perhaps sixteen. She was bareheaded, and her blonde hair was cropped short about her face, which increased her resemblance to a creature invisible to normal human vision. Her features were delicate: a nose so small it could almost, but not quite, be condemned as snub, a modest but generously lipped mouth, pretty little ears exposed by her haircut, a pointed chin, grey eyes with an almost startled look in them. It was an ethereal and genuine beauty—in debt to nature, not Elizabeth Arden.

He could not judge her height on horseback but saw that she was slender and held her back ramrod straight. He stood waiting for her to speak, to hear how eldritch voices sounded and what they said. She swung her torso suddenly down, so that it seemed inevitable that she must pitch off the horse's back head first, retrieved a hard hat from where it had fallen on the ground and straightened gracefully up again. Nick felt like applauding. She put the hat back on, pressing it down hard so that it only just cleared her eyes.

"Is Mrs. Bottone at home?" he asked. "Laura?"

She nodded, pointed to the house, and turned away from him again, urging Golden Wonder into a brisk trot and then a canter. Nick turned regretfully away. Could this be the "rather dim sort of stable girl" described by Alison? If so, what a pity. He didn't go to the front door this time but went straight into the yard to the open back door. "Nick?" Laura called out, rising from her seat, pleased. "Come on in." He advanced into the kitchen where Amy was playing some childish card game on the floor and Patience was jumbling up the cards as she went along.

"I've brought your address book back."

"Oh, thank you." She stretched out her hand and took it from him, her finger tips just brushing his own. "You haven't got to rush off?"

"By no means." He sat down and asked casually, "Who's that out in the paddock on Golden Wonder?"

"Oh, that's my eldest daughter, Edwina Rutherford." Nick winced. "Edwin Rutherford was a very vain man," she added.

"I didn't realize you'd been married before."

"Edwin was killed in a car accident in Italy. We were living out there then." She laughed at him. "I know what you're thinking, Chief Inspector, that to lose one husband may be an accident but to lose two begins to look like carelessness."

"A sad misfortune, certainly."

"Perhaps I'm just a bad picker."

"Was that where you met Arturo, when you were living out in Italy?"

She nodded. "He was our handyman cum chauffeur cum gardener. Edwin was a rich man, you see; he owned quite an estate out near Palma, vineyards and all. Arturo was actually quite a comfort when Edwin died, and I suppose I must have been in my Lady Chatterley mood at the time. Edwin left everything to me, including these stables. We hung around in Italy for a few months, but the place held too many bad memories for me and I sold up and came here."

"Edwina's a superb horsewoman," Nick said, reverting to his good fairy, "not that I know anything about it, but you couldn't tell where she ended and the horse began."

Laura looked pleased. "I taught her. I think she's good;

she's the only person apart from me that's allowed to exercise Goldie."

"How old is she, as a matter of interest?"

"Sixteen. She's been away at boarding school for the past few years, but she's not very academic so she didn't want to stay on past this summer when she reached the school-leaving age."

"Not academic!" Felicity chimed in. "That's a good one. You've heard of the princess and the pea, Uncle Nick? Well, she's Princess Peabrain."

"I couldn't get a word out of her," Nick said. "Is she very shy?"

Laura shrugged apologetically. "Some people"—she glared at Felicity—"think she's a bit thick, but it's more that she's not very good with humans, prefers to talk to horses any day. She wants to be a jockey, so she's helping out round here for the summer while we try to find a stable willing to take her. I have friends in the business. I think we'll find something to suit." She patted the address book. "That's one of the reasons I wanted this back."

"You haven't, um, had any nasty phone calls, have you?" Nick asked. He had three aims in this visit: to return the book, to ask this question and to see these new friends again.

"Phone calls? No. Why?" He explained about Deborah Tyson. Laura sighed. "Poor woman."

"No poorer than you," he pointed out. "In fact less so: she still has her husband, fallen and disgraced as she sees him to be."

"I told you before," Laura's back stiffened and she leaned away from him, "I don't need pity. Action, not self-pity—that's what's needed in a crisis."

"You're not getting any pity from me. I can't think of anyone who needs it less."

She unbent a little. "I wonder why these nuisances picked on her rather than me; I'd be so much better able to cope with it."

"Perhaps that's why. Anyway, this is a long way to come to put excrement through your door."

"Don't you just love the human race, in all its slimy small-mindedness?" Laura said after a pause.

"How was the film?" Nick asked Alison when she got home that night.

"Oh, we had a change of heart, decided it was too hot for anything so cerebral. Went to see a couple of old spaghetti Westerns instead." He made a derisive noise. "I thought they were quite interesting," she said.

"*A Fistful of Dollars?* Well, that should just suit you. With your tame Americans in tow this summer."

"Always room for a few dollars more," she said.

13

Mr. Tyson was not pleased to see Nick when he finally caught up with him the next day. He was even less pleased to see Humbleby with his inevitable camera.

"I'm not allowed to have visitors in my room," he muttered, looking back through the door of the hostel to see if anyone was listening, "and you're not taking any photos, whoever you are."

"Mr. Humbleby is on loan to us from the, er, Home Office," Nick improvised.

"I don't care if he's Lord Lichfield. No photos. Haven't I had enough to put up with? My name splashed all over the front of the local paper?" Well, that was one way of describing a small paragraph on page six, Nick thought. "The address of my house blazoned for every snooper in the valley to come and stare at it." Nick refrained from pointing out that it was Deborah Tyson who was suffering as a result of this.

"A little walk along the cliff?" he suggested. "It's such a lovely day."

Tyson pulled the door shut behind him and shuffled down the road with them. He looked ten years older than he had that day in the park, little more than a week ago; he hadn't shaved for a few days, and his clothes were grubby and creased.

"I'm not very good with housework," he said, following Nick's eyes, "ironing, and all that. Deborah does that."

"I don't suppose the facilities are very good in the hostel," Nick said tactfully.

"No. That's right. It's not what I'm used to." He gained confidence, grew more aggressive. "I don't know what you want. I've been to court and been fined and bound over or whatever it was. I'm having to see a bloody psychiatrist like I was some sort of bloody loony. Isn't that enough for you? I don't have to talk to you any more."

"I saw your wife," Nick said. "Deborah. She's in a bad way."

"What's the matter with her?"

"Trouble with the neighbors, obscene and threatening phone calls." Nick was pulling no punches.

"Jesus!" They reached the cliff top and Wesley Tyson sat down heavily on a bench. "I didn't know. She's not talking to me at the moment—not about anything that matters."

"She's near the end of her tether." Nick sat down beside him. Jim wandered away and began to photograph the scenery.

"So, why are you telling me all this?" Tyson asked. "Just to make me feel good?"

"Just to keep you going to that bloody psychiatrist, to get yourself sorted out, get back home where you belong, taking care of her."

"I see." Tyson stared out to sea for a moment. Sailing boats glided along the sheltered coastline, their occupiers calling happily to each other in the un-English heat. The warmth made people more relaxed, more openhearted. It all looked so normal and right. "I tried to fight it. For years. I've never *touched* a kid, you know. Never had the guts. I love Deborah. I love my kids. It was just . . . I dunno . . . like a madness."

"You're lucky in a way, that it's been caught in time," Nick said. "Before you did turn your fantasies into reality with some little girl or boy."

"Boy!" Tyson was affronted. "I'm not a fucking queer!"

They said that everyone needed someone to look down on: for men who fancied little girls, apparently, it was men who fancied little boys.

"You can be helped," Nick said. "I firmly believe that."

"I suppose I should be grateful." He glanced sideways at Nick. "Although I didn't see it that way at the time. When you arrested me, I was so scared I would be sent to prison I was almost shitting myself. It brought me to my senses. I'd never have gone for help otherwise. What is it you want to know?"

"Just small things: like how you met Bottone in the first place."

"There are adverts," Tyson said readily, "in the normal porno mags, the adult ones that you get in the corner newsagents. Or even in *Health and Efficiency.* If you look carefully, read between the lines, you can see the ones which are offering 'specialized services for the more so-phisticated taste,' magazines for the 'Young at Heart.'"

"That makes sense."

"You send off, not committing yourself, just saying you might be interested in anything out of the ordinary they have. They're equally circumspect. You use a false name, make sure you get to the post before your wife does so she doesn't start asking who this Bill Smithson is who's getting his post sent to your house. Or you get them sent to your office marked 'strictly private and personal.'"

Nick listened, fascinated.

"After a suitable exchange of caginess, you might buy some magazines by post—using a postal order, of course, not your own check. I used one firm in London for the last couple of years, then two, three months ago they wrote and said they could put me in touch with someone working in my area if I wanted to deal with him direct, said it would be safer." He laughed bitterly. "Safer! I meet him once to place my order, as it were. The first time I go to collect, there you are."

"Can I have the name of this firm you dealt with by post?" Nick asked. Tyson recited by heart an address in an amorphous suburb of West London—Heston or Hanwell or Hounslow. Nick wrote it down.

"That was just magazines, though," he explained. "One of the reasons I was so pleased about dealing with the dago was that he promised me photos, real ones, recent ones." He looked regretful. "I never even saw them." Nick, who had and wished he hadn't, felt his heart harden towards this little man, with his facade of respectability—his veneer of wife and kids and job and mortgage—stripped away.

Tyson turned to look out to sea again. "Do you despise me?"

"I suppose I do rather. Pity you, but also despise you."

"That's honest! Dr. Frobisher's spent the last few days explaining to me how I'm not despicable, and I know deep down he thinks I am. Suppose I were to tell you that my dad left home when I was three and that my mother had a string of blokes about the place after that. That I never knew from one day to the next whether it was going to be

Uncle George or Uncle Bob today? That Mum used to make me get into bed with the pair of them, whichever Uncle it was? That I had to let them play with me unless I wanted a walloping? What would you say then?"

"I would say: Is it the truth?"

"Perhaps. Or perhaps not. Perhaps it's just an idea Dr. Frobisher put into my head. Who knows?"

"You can be helped," Nick said again, "But you have to want to be helped. Not just to play games with Dr. Frobisher and see how gullible he can be."

"Sharp, aren't you?" Tyson turned his cunning eyes on Nick, who saw no repentance in them.

"I have a built-in bullshit detector," he said. "Now, how about it? For Deborah's sake."

"All right," Tyson said. "For Deborah's sake, and my kids. I'll give it a try."

"This is delicious, Alison." Humbleby waved his forkful of chicken in the air. "Really delicious."

"Nick made it," was all Alison replied. She was not overjoyed to have a member of the press foisted on her in her own home despite Nick's assurances that Jim was different. "More cabbage?"

"No thanks. Not a big greens man, probably why I didn't grow up big and strong like Popeye. Ha ha. You know"— he had been staring at Alison periodically ever since his arrival—"you look very familiar. Haven't I seen your picture in the *Financial Times?*"

"Only you can answer that question," she replied sweetly.

"Oh! See what you mean!" He giggled.

"Why are you being so rude to him?" Nick hissed as they

met up in the kitchen while she was making coffee; he was loading the dishwasher and Humbleby had been safely disposed of in a deckchair on the terrace.

"Never trust a man who wears a cardigan—"

"Good God, Alison! Talk about prejudice."

"And never trust a man who won't eat up his greens."

"Now you're being ridiculous."

"I'm serious." Alison assumed a lecturing stance, wagging her finger at him. "It's my observation, over a period of many years, that men who won't eat up their cabbage are stuck in adolescence. Children never like vegetables, but it's something normal people grow out of. Those who don't, usually men, are emotionally retarded; it's a sure sign. I bet he's a trainspotter."

Nick made an exasperated noise and slammed shut the door of the dishwasher with uncalled-for force. There was a sound of something smashing inside but neither of them took any notice.

"And he doesn't drink," she said, clinching the argument as far as she was concerned. "Whoever heard of a journalist who doesn't drink?"

"One of us had better go and be civil to our guest." He left the room.

"You patronize him!" she called after him.

As she laid the tray of coffee and brandy carefully down on the stone parapet a few minutes later, Jim Humbleby was saying, "I hear there's quite a famous steamtrain runs from Bishop's Lydeard to Minehead. I might give myself a few hours off some time to go and take a ride on it."

Nick suppressed a snort and would not meet her eye. "I'm sure that'll be great fun," he said.

Humbleby took as many photos of the interior of Hope

Cottage as she would permit. Nick grew a little worried—
he didn't want people looking at Alison's elaborate drawing room and inferring that chief inspectors were grossly
overpaid.

"Hope Cottage belongs to Alison," he reminded him
more than once. "I have a little—well, tiny really—flat in
town."

The reporter was effusive in his thanks as he left at about
eleven, Nick offering to run him back to his hotel since he
didn't drive.

"Hope to see more of you," he called to Alison, who was
standing on the doorstep to make sure he really left.

"This is all there is of me," she called back.

"Great sense of humor," Humbleby said, as they pulled
out onto the main road. "I like that in a woman."

14

Nick was lying awake in bed that night. It was two o'clock and the windows out onto the balcony were wide open, but it was still too hot to sleep. Alison dozed fitfully at his side, muttering occasionally. He was almost glad when the telephone gave that staccato hiccup which announced that it was about to ring. He snatched it up before the first trill and said quietly, "Trevellyan."

"It's Shirley. We've had an arson attack."

"Give me a second." Nick sat up; he was already sliding out of bed. The telephone was on a long lead and he took it into the bathroom, shut the door, turned the light on and sat down on the lavatory seat.

"Shirley?"

"Sorry to wake you."

"You didn't. Arson, you say? There's a novelty. I can't remember the last arson we had. Someone feeling the cold?"

"It's in Dove Crescent—"

"Don't tell me. Number eight."

"How did you know that?"

"I am omniscient, Sergeant. I thought you knew that."

"Yes, sir."

"Is anyone hurt?"

"The occupier's been taken to hospital suffering from smoke inhalation, but I think she's going to be all right. There didn't seem to be anyone else in the house. The fire brigade's got the blaze under control; there's a lot of damage to furniture, curtains and so on, but nothing too structural, as far as I can make out."

"How did it start?"

"Looks like a rag with petrol on it was pushed through the letter box, then a lighted spill chucked in after. Most of the damage is to the hall and stairs."

"Where are you?"

"At the scene. I took the liberty of using their phone."

"Sounds like you've got everything under control."

"I can carry on, if you prefer. I just thought you'd like to be informed, as it's such a serious crime."

"No, you did right. I'm on my way."

"All the neighbors are awake, but they're curiously unhelpful."

"Don't you recognize the address? After all," he added, twisting the knife, "you were the one in court that fateful day."

"Shit! Tyson."

"Be with you in ten minutes."

He hung up, dressed, left a scrawled note for Alison, who had not stirred, and let himself silently out of the house.

It was the middle of the night. Hortense was teething. She was not exactly crying, just grizzling. Lucy could hear her through the open doors, but she could not summon up the energy to get out of bed. Dragged back from sleep against her will, she felt as if she were coming up from an intolerable depth of water. She wished there were someone next to her so she could roll over and poke him in the ribs and say, "Your turn tonight."

Let her cry. It couldn't hurt. There were times when she wanted to cry herself. If anything, she felt better after.

The grizzling escalated to a wail. It was no good. Easy does it. Lucy slid one foot out from under the sheet and put it on the floor, her toes flexed against the bare wood. Almost there. The other foot followed slowly; the body was heaved upwards in one final thrusting motion. The wailing became sobbing. Lucy was finally on her feet, naked, walking across the landing.

"It's all right, precious. Mummy's here."

She picked her up. Hungry? Wet? She felt. Wet. The sky was clear and the moon full; she did not need to switch on the light. She changed the nappy clumsily—it had not become second nature to her, and more talcum powder seemed to coat the floor rather than Hortense's golden body—but the baby was satisfied with her efforts and, cradled in her warm arms, began to gurgle.

Lucy stood rocking her, looking out towards the sea. There was not another house, another human soul in sight. She and her daughter were alone in the world.

"So we're assuming it's not a random attack," Shirley said.

"No," Nick agreed, "it's someone lashing out. It's part of a pattern of revenge on the Tysons." He explained about the telephone calls and the previous unwelcome gifts through the letter box.

"Sir?"

A voice behind him made Nick turn round. He recognized a newish and ambitious young constable who called his superiors "sir" far too often.

"Constable Fisher. Is this your beat?"

"Yes, sir."

"I gave orders that a special watch was to be kept on this house."

"Yes, sir. That's why I'm here now, sir."

"Too late, Fisher. Too late."

The young man looked sulky. "I have got a whole beat to do, sir. I can't be everywhere at once."

"All right. I know."

"I was trying to route myself round here at least once an hour, but I got an emergency call. False alarm too, sir."

"Oh? Tell Me."

"999 call passed on—report of a domestic in Selborne Road. Said they weren't sure if it was number thirty-nine or number forty-one. It was all quiet there, and by the time I'd checked it out and got back here, sir—" He waved his arm at the smoking mess of number eight, Dove Crescent.

"Now wasn't that convenient?" Shirley remarked. "A nine nine nine call just at the wrong time, and a false alarm to boot."

"I think we'll have a listen to the recording," Nick agreed. "Our man is no fool. Except that he may not realize that emergency calls are taped and probably won't have done anything to disguise his voice."

"All right, Des," Shirley said to Fisher, "you needn't wait."

"Sarge!"

"Oh, and Fisher?" Nick said.

"Sir!"

"Don't call me 'sir' every thirty seconds."

Fisher, to his credit, did not answer, "Yes, sir," but after a short pause said, "Right you are then" and left.

"You can go in now." The Chief Fire Officer came towards them through the front garden, which was no longer neat and well stocked but trampled underfoot by half a dozen firemen and their equipment. No chance of any footprints there. "I think it's safe," he added.

"He *thinks* it's safe," Nick muttered as he and Shirley pushed open the front door, which sagged sadly off its hinges where it had been broken down to gain access, and looked into the hall. "Oh God!"

"It's not as bad as it looks," Shirley ventured. "Most of the mess is the water from the hoses."

"How do they manage to do more damage than the fire itself every time?" Nick asked.

"Shh! They'll hear you."

"Where are the SOCOs?"

"On their way."

Nick stepped carefully over the burned rag on what remained of the doormat and stood in the hall with his hands in his pockets, staring up the stairs. The flowered wallpaper was curling off the walls; the carpet was sodden where it wasn't charred. The hall stand was matchwood and the potted plant past succor. There was soot everywhere.

"This is going to be the last straw," he said. "Poor bloody Deborah."

Poor Deborah Tyson: she had done nothing, committed no crime; but husband and wife were one flesh, even in these days of easy divorce, and what her husband had done, she would pay for.

"She could have been killed," he said. "I want this treated as attempted murder, Shirley."

She looked surprised. "If you say so."

"Yes, get an incident room set up first thing. Get all the uniformed help you need. I'll answer for it to the superintendent, if necessary."

He was interested to learn that the man who felt so strongly about the kiddy porn did not confine himself to the cowardly route of telephone calls and fecal parcels. He was prepared to kill.

Part Two

A child's a plaything for an hour.

Mary Lamb
Parental Recollections

1

There was something touching about Lucy's cottage; it was like the realization of a dream. It was old, very old; pink-washed, thatched, with windows so small that little light could penetrate. There was evidence of recent renovation in the form of fresh paintwork. It stood isolated on a small promontory in overgrown gardens without another dwelling in sight.

Nick reached it at the end of a long road—little more than a cart track which must be very muddy in winter but was now a dust bowl. The track turned uphill for the last hundred yards, and as he reached the topmost point of the hillock, he had a clear view to the sea about half a mile away. In the summer sun, it looked idyllic.

He parked next to a newish Citroen 2CV, parti-colored in yellow and grey and with a child seat in the rear. He had not known Lucy owned a car, had not even known she could drive; but you couldn't really live out in the wilds like this without transport. It looked as if she was at home, which was lucky, as he had not rung first; he had been passing that way coming back from Hopcliff and, seeing the turnoff with the signpost to High Wind, had decided to try his luck.

He remembered to leave his car windows open. There had been too many days lately when he had come back to it to find the seat unbearably sticky, the steering wheel too hot to hold. The front door stood open and he tapped on it and called out, "Lucy?"

"Come in." The voice came from somewhere at the back and he blundered on, blinded by the sudden transition from heatwave to shaded interior. Purple and brown patches of light seemed to curve away from him in all directions like fleeing goblins.

"I wasn't expecting you back so soon," the voice continued, coming closer, then, "Nick! It's you."

"I hope it's not inconvenient."

"Of course not."

His eyes were now accustoming themselves to the gloom, and he could make out Lucy standing in a doorway at the other end of the hall with Hortense cradled over her shoulder in the burping position. "Come on through," she said, backing away before him. "I've just finished feeding her."

"Don't tell me," Nick said, following. "I bet you've got an Aga and an inglenook and beams."

"Mind your head."

He ducked under a low lintel into the kitchen, which did have beams but no Aga. Instead it had an old electric cooker and some rather shabby units topped with formica.

"The gentlemen were old-fashioned," she explained. "They had everything kitted out new sometime just after the war. They'd had enough messing about with lighting fires when they were young; they voted for electric logs and easy-wipe plastic every time." She waved her free hand at the units. "These were the bees knees some time around nineteen fifty-three."

"Delightful."

"But I did find these under the lino." She indicated the flagstones on the floor. There was a thick blanket folded under the table and she put Hortense down on it. The baby rolled over on her stomach and kicked her legs. "And there is an inglenook in the sitting room, although it had been cunningly hidden."

"It's lovely, Lucy." Now that he could see her properly, he saw that she was tired and that, despite her usual banter, she had forgotten to smile. He wanted to strike a positive note. In fact the house struck him as neglected and sad.

"It will be. I shall be getting the kitchen redone, of course. There's a lot to do, but I'm in no hurry. I've got years and years to do it in. Coffee?" He accepted and took a seat at the table. "There is a place we can sit out at the back," she said, "like a terrace, but it's a bit too hot for Hortense this early in the afternoon. She'll go down for her sleep soon, with a bit of luck."

"Were you expecting someone else?" Nick asked, suddenly struck by her greeting of him.

"Oh." She turned away to pour coffee from a filter machine. "Just a friend."

"Male friend?" She nodded, handing him his mug. "I see."

"It's not like that. The way I feel at the moment, I doubt if I shall ever get turned on again."

Nick was all at sea. Childbirth—its problems and pleasures, its sudden swings of mood—was outside his experience. "Did you have a, um, difficult labor?" he asked, not sure that he wanted to hear the details.

"Not too bad actually, considering. The stitches have healed up properly and everything. It isn't physical; I just can't remember why I ever wanted to bother with sex."

"What's the problem?"

"I'm finding it hard work, motherhood. And admitting it is the hardest part."

"Didn't you know it would be?"

"In theory. I thought I was ready for it. I thought I could cope. I shall be forty next birthday, and this seemed like my last chance. God knows, girls of seventeen and younger cope. I was prepared for the disturbed nights, for the loss of libido—not that I've got anyone to libid with at the moment—and a little depression. I wasn't prepared for the loneliness."

"But you've always had so many friends," he reminded her.

"That's what I thought. One whiff of Napisan is enough to drive them away apparently." She sat down at the table opposite him and wiped her face wearily with a disposable nappy. "And it's so bloody hot all the time, I feel like my brain doesn't function properly. I can't remember what it's like to feel cold, just like I can't remember what it's like to feel randy. Whenever I think I'll take Hortense for a walk to the sea in her buggy, I get fifty yards and all the energy just seeps away."

"I'm here. I'm not allergic to Napisan." He squeezed her arm.

"Thanks, Nick."

"And you have this other friend. Anyone I know?"

She shook her head. "His name's Ryder—Ryder Drew. He's a photographer."

"Indeed?" Nick's ears pricked up at the word.

"He lives in London but he's been touring round here a lot lately."

"So he does landscape photography? Wildlife?"

118

"No. Fashion mostly." She peered proudly under the table at her offspring. "He thinks Hortense might make a model."

"Oh?"

"It seems that black babies are fashionable at the moment."

"Especially if they're not *too* black," he suggested.

"Mmm. Maybe."

"I wouldn't have thought it was your sort of thing at all, Lucy."

"Why not? Why shouldn't Hortense be a successful model? What have I done with my life? Wasted it away teaching French to uninterested kids in a school in a small town for almost twenty years."

Nick was momentarily taken aback; this sounded so unlike the Lucy Fielding he knew. "I thought that was your choice."

"Oh! I had such plans once . . ."

He thought for a moment that she might cry and hastened to comfort her. "You've always been one of the best liked and most respected teachers at the Comprehensive. You know you have. You've inspired generations of students. How can that be a waste?" He was worried now. She had always been so hardheaded, he knew, so certain. Some had called her cynical. But she had the usual mother's blind spot where her baby was concerned, only too willing to believe that she was the most beautiful baby in the world—a budding model. She sniffled a bit, then took a pile of catalogs out of the drawer in front of her and plonked them on the table.

"See. Just children's clothes and toys. That sort of thing."

Nick picked up one marked "Everything for the mother-to-be and children up to ten." He leafed through the first few pages. There were indeed babies no older than Hortense modeling romper suits, Babygros, christening frocks. They were solemn in push chairs and playpens, bald in tot wheels and high chairs, laughing in plastic baths marked *Baby*. Few were as naturally pretty as Hortense.

"Look at this," Lucy said eagerly. "This" was a Lullaby Bunny: it was voice-activated so that when the baby woke up and cried, its cheeks would glow in the dark and a soothing lullaby would play. It was available in pink or blue and had squinty little eyes and a bored expression. "Isn't it sweet?"

"Mmm." Did motherhood do away with good taste, he wondered? Did hormonal surges really create a liking for this vulgar artifact? He hardly recognized his bright, funny, forceful friend.

Farther on there were older children in jeans, trainers, jogging suits. Little girls in party frocks and, surely, a touch of lipstick looked provocatively out at the camera, holding hands with adults. Flat-chested eight-year-olds modeled bikinis. Boys were mock-tough in cotton briefs, pretending to flex nonexistent muscles as if they were not really helpless and vulnerable in an adult world. One girl in shorts and ankle socks held up her face to a man to be kissed. All the children were blond except for one mixed-race child, and all the girls had long curls. There was something unpleasantly knowing about them; and something pathetic too. He turned back to the babies.

"That's the sort of thing Ryder has in mind for Hortense," Lucy said. "He says she's bound to be very photogenic."

"I'm sure."

"He's very good with children; she seems to trust him. He took a few sample shots and when he put her in position she just stayed there as good as gold, as if she knew he wanted to make her a star." She smiled remembrance. She had not been quite truthful earlier. She had someone to "libid" with in her sights, if only as a blur on the horizon at present.

"So, when are you expecting Ryder back? I'd love to meet him."

"Really?" She accepted the remark at face value. "He said he'd drop by with the test photos he took and discuss a full portfolio, probably later this week."

"I shall drop in again then, if I may." He hesitated. "I don't know how to put this, Lucy, but are you sure this bloke's legit?"

She looked hurt and he felt ashamed. "I don't know what you mean. He's got cameras, business cards. He brought all the gear with him. You should have seen her in a christening robe; she looked like a little princess."

"Hardly your sort of thing, though."

"Funnily enough, I had been meaning to ask you if you would be her godfather."

Nick was astonished. "Isn't that all a bit . . . establishment for you?"

"Maybe. But she's got very little family, you see. My only living relatives aren't even in England. What am I saying? They aren't even in Europe."

"And she certainly won't know her father's family."

"Let's not go over that again. I thought it would be nice if she had some godparents to give her presents on her birthday, take her to the pantomime."

"Sounds like the whole affair's going to be a pantomime." He sounded unnecessarily harsh, even to his own ears, but he pressed on. "I'm sorry, Lucy, I can't do it. I have no religious beliefs, as you know, and I didn't think you did either."

"You take the oath in court," she pointed out. "I've heard you."

"I have enough trouble getting the jury to believe my side of the story without setting myself up as a card-carrying atheist, thanks very much."

"So, what's the difference?"

"That I have too much respect for you to make vows in church that are meaningless to me. Let me be a sort of honorary uncle, a secular godfather. I'll buy her presents, take her out."

She sighed. "I just thought I'd ask."

"You could ask Alison. She collects godchildren and she's very generous to them."

She looked defiant. "I might even do that. Or perhaps I shall ask Ryder."

He glanced at his watch. "I really can't stay any longer, Lucy. I shouldn't have been here this long. I've got a crisis on. Arson, would you believe? But I'll be back soon, perhaps at the weekend."

"Yeah." She stood despondently by the door as he backed out of the front garden. She waved.

"Thanks for looking in."

Jim, sorry to have missed out on the previous night's excitement, was making up for it today.

"You should have woken me," he complained to Shirley, snapping away at the exterior and interior of the house, getting in the way of the police photographer and the SO-COs and trampling the flower beds yet further.

"You wouldn't say that if you'd been called out in the middle of the night as often as I have," she told him.

"So what now?"

"I'm setting up a mobile incident room on the corner of the street. That should be here any minute now. Then people who live round here and might have seen something can drop in on their way home from work."

"That sounds exciting."

"No, Jim," she said patiently. "It'll just be a lot of constables taking a lot of statements. Paperwork, paperwork, and then more paperwork. Then I'm setting up house-to-house inquiries, again with the help of uniformed branch. That'll go on far into the evening as well, since half the houses are unoccupied by day."

"And where's the Chief Inspector got to? I haven't seen him today."

"He's gone to break the news to Mr. Tyson at that hostel in Hopcliff." She looked at her watch. "I thought he'd've been back by now."

Jim, in his element, put a new roll of film in his camera and carried on snapping.

2

"Emergency. Which service do you require?"

"Police."

The voice was quiet, almost a whisper. The man knew, as Nick did, that a whispered voice is harder to identify—somehow dehumanized, often unsexed. Even so, Nick, playing the recording through for the fourth time, thought he recognized the speech patterns, the local accent, of the man he had spoken to on Mrs. Tyson's telephone two days before the arson attack. He played on as the call was put through to Hopbridge police station and WPC Greenslade's voice was recognizable in the control room.

"Police. Can I help you?"

"There's a bit of a barney going on in Selborne Road. A domestic. I'm not sure which number—"

"May I have your name please, sir?"

"It's one of the two semis with red doors about half way along. Thirty-nine or forty-one, I think."

Myra Greenslade persevered. "I must have your name please, sir."

"Look, sweetheart. There's a bloke knocking seven bells out of his missus and you waste time asking me my name. I'm just a bystander, okay? I don't wanna get involved. Selborne Road, half way up, side nearest the main road. Okay?"

He had hung up then. The call had been relayed to PC Fisher, despite the lack of detail, and Fisher had found it to be a false alarm; either that, or the man had finished knocking seven bells out of his wife and decided against an eighth.

"The line was held open, of course," Shirley said, "while they traced it, but it turned out to be a call box on the corner of Bridgwater Drive. Just round the corner from Dove Crescent, in other words. It's one of the new type without a door, and there were more fingerprints on the receiver and dial than there are pebbles on Hop-mouth beach."

"Get our own copy, will you?" Nick said. "And ask our people to get rid of as much background noise as possible. I may need this in court."

"The same man? You recognize his voice?"

"I'd bet a year's salary on it."

He talked Humbleby through the exhibits they were gathering in the arson case.

"Have you got many, um, suspects?" Jim asked.

"It doesn't quite work like that, I'm afraid." Nick took him into the collator's room where records of local criminals were held. "We've no one locally with a record for arson; besides, there's arson and there's arson."

"How d'you mean?"

"True arsonists torch buildings for the love of it."

"Pyromaniacs? I like a good bonfire myself."

"Then there's arson for gain—usually insurance fraud—and arson as a means of personal attack, as in the Tyson case. Sadly, that seems to be getting more frequent but usually as a racial attack, which, thank God, we don't get much of round here."

"I get it. So the chances are the person who started the fire has never committed arson before."

"Very good, Jim."

"He might just as easily have waylaid Mr. Tyson one dark night and given him a good hiding."

"He might."

"So how can you hope to find him?"

"Forensic is our best bet. We're still sifting through the wreckage, very slowly. Then we have that voice, on tape, which I believe is that of the arsonist."

Nick went to the hospital later that morning to find Mike Brewster, who ought to have had some reports back from the pathology laboratory by now. He came across the doctor cozily tucked up in his office drinking coffee with David Hazlett-Jones.

"You remember Davey, of course."

"Of course." The two men shook hands again. Hazlett-Jones looked vaguely embarrassed and fiddled a good deal with his moustache. "Well, I mustn't get in your way," he said, the moment Nick arrived. "You have business to discuss."

"Finish your coffee for God's sake, Davey," Mike said. "Nick won't mind. How's the great pervert hunt going, Nick?"

"Not well," Nick replied cautiously.

"No names from among the great and the good—or not-so-good—of Hopbridge yet?"

"Not yet, but there will be." He would have preferred it if Hazlett-Jones left, but he could hardly bundle the man out. He introduced Jim and explained who he was, and the two doctors expressed polite interest in the project.

"If we get a PM to do during your stay, you must get Nick to bring you," Brewster said with a straight face.

"I'd like that."

"No," Nick said, "you wouldn't."

"Can I take your photos?" Jim asked.

"Well." Dr Hazlett-Jones gulped down the rest of his coffee so fast he almost choked on it. "Work to do, work to do. Smear tests don't do themselves. Nice to meet you, Mr. . . . erm." He gave up trying to remember Jim's name and concluded, "Regards to Alison."

"What's the matter with him?" Nick asked after the gynecologist had left.

Mike shrugged. "He was fine until you arrived. I thought he was set to stay all morning, in fact. Then he suddenly starts acting like a man with a guilty conscience. Funny the effect you fuzz have on even the most law-abiding citizens." He flapped his hand at Humbleby, who was hovering. "Yes, if you like, but I warn you, I'm not photogenic." He struck a pose, avuncular behind his desk in his white coat.

"So, what have you got for me?" Nick asked, dismissing Davey Jones's odd behavior from his mind.

"Alcohol, as I thought. No other drugs have been identified."

"There were certainly plenty of empty bottles at the scene."

"He had something like six, seven times the legal limit for driving in his bloodstream."

"That sounds an awful lot," Jim said in awe.

"Say three bottles of wine. I'm slightly surprised he hadn't passed out at that level, but you can never tell; it affects people in different ways."

Nick said, "Are you seriously suggesting he might have been sufficiently *compos mentis* to tie a knot in a leading rein, get up on the chair, tie it to the beam—all with that amount of booze inside him?"

"You're not still harping on the possibility that it wasn't suicide, surely," Mike said impatiently. "Anything is possible. He might have set the noose up before he started drinking. Then downed a lot of wine very quickly to give himself the courage, started to hang himself while it was still coursing into his bloodstream. It's not quick, you know, hanging. Not the homemade variety."

"I know. You've had more experience than I have, Mike. Don't they usually have a last-minute change of heart, start clawing at the rope before losing consciousness, or something?"

"Ugh!" Humbleby said. "I thought it was instantaneous, like after the judge puts his black cap on and they give you a hearty breakfast."

"In judicial hanging the weight of the person being hanged is taken into account and the drop carefully calculated," Nick explained. "Then they put weights on his legs so that the neck snaps as soon as the noose tightens."

"Thanks, Nick. I've just lost any desire I previously had for lunch."

"Nick. . . ," Dr. Brewster said, "I'd like to be able to say that there was something wrong if it'll make you happy, but, really, there was nothing inconsistent with all the other hangings I've dealt with in my time."

"All right."

"Although to answer your question about the last-minute

change of heart: yes, it does happen. But Bottone's nails were bitten down to the quick, so they wouldn't have left any lasting trace if he had."

"Damn. I noticed his nails but then I forgot."

"People will do almost anything under stress, you know." Mike Brewster was very fond of diagnoses of stress, Nick had noticed—that and obscure allergies. He sometimes thought if you went to him with a broken leg he'd say you were allergic to falling off the roof.

"So, drop it," the doctor was saying. "Are you short of something to do, or what? I thought I heard something in the town about an arson attack."

"That's just it." Nick explained about the fire at the Tysons' house. "If Bottone committed suicide, he did an awful lot of people a big favor."

Laura held Benjie's head while Alison slipped her feet from the stirrups and alighted. "I think we can graduate you to something a little more challenging next time," she said gravely.

"How about Golden Wonder?" Alison asked.

"No chance." The two women stood smiling at each other. They had liked each other on sight. Each of them was blessed with a quiet strength, a commanding will, and admired these qualities in others. Edwina appeared and began to lead Benjie away towards the paddock. She didn't say a word to either woman. Laura called after her.

"Edwina. Can you take Brimstone into the stable and worm him when you've done Benjie. He's about due. I want him at his peak for the gymkhana. You know what store Feckless sets by getting the red rosette this year after she was so disappointed last time." Edwina gave one of her rare smiles and nodded. As Alison watched, she deftly removed Benjie's saddle and began to rub him down. "She and Feckless are devoted to each other," Laura said. "Feckless makes fun of her all the time, but she's very protective of her. Daft, really, with her being so much younger, but she treats Edwina like a silly kid sister."

Alison could see why. Her few attempts to make conversation with Edwina had been conspicuous failures. Either she did not reply at all or her remarks were so banal or fatuous that the effort of responding to them made Alison's head ache.

"What happened last year?" she asked as Edwina let Benjie loose in the paddock and called to Brimstone, who came instantly to hand at the promise of a few horse nuts and let the bridle be slipped over his head.

"She was in the final jump-off against the clock, having been one of three kids with clear rounds. Last summer was quite wet, if you remember, and Brimstone slipped on a patch of mud just before the last fence and fell right into it, practically demolished it. That put paid to her chances." Alison made sympathetic noises. "She came third, got a yellow rosette, but it's not the same, is it?"

Alison agreed heartily that it was not. Coming in first was something she felt strongly about.

"She was the youngest competitor in the twelve-and-under too," Laura added. "Only eight then. Most of them were great galumphing girls of about eleven. Come in and have some tea if you've got time."

"I've got time. Aren't you busy?"

"Business has slackened off a little since . . . well, I expect you've heard what happened."

Alison nodded. "I wanted to offer my sympathy, but somehow it never seemed the right moment."

Laura brushed the condolence away. "So, some of the parents have stopped bringing their children, canceled lessons at short notice."

"That must be a blow. And so unfair."

"Oh, they'll be back. This is the only stable for miles around, and the local schools break up today. The kids will soon get bored and start nagging to be back in the saddle."

"I do know what it's like," Alison ventured, "when something like this happens and the police are swarming all over the place. Something very similar happened to me three years ago."

"Really? You must tell me about it." She began to lead Alison across the yard towards the house. Brimstone was now trotting demurely behind Edwina in the direction of the stable. He held his handsome head up and strained forward with an evident desire to please.

"He trots beautifully to hand," Laura remarked, "but Feckless won't enter him in the leading-rein competitions. She says that's kid's stuff and jumping's the only thing worth competing in for a serious equestrienne."

Just as horse and handler reached the threshold, the ginger tomcat came jogging out with what looked like an adolescent rat struggling in his mouth. Suddenly Brimstone was up on his hind legs, neighing desperately, as if in panic, his hooves pounding the air. The ginger tom howled, dropped the rodent, and streaked back into the stable with his head down and his tail flat behind him like a golden bullet. The young rat looked round in disbelief, then made good its escape. The pony jerked his rein out of Edwina's surprised hand and backed away from the stable door on his hind legs before going back on all fours. He bolted away to his left, back past the paddock, heading for the gate which led out of the stable yard, out onto the moors. His head pumped up and down; his eyes were wide with terror.

The five-bar gate was shut.

Alison had not known she could run so fast. Laura was just behind her calling out, "Not the gate. Don't let him try to jump the gate. He'll kill himself."

Brimstone was quickening his stride now, galloping full out, all set to try to take the gate, which was much too high for a twelve-hand pony. Alison hadn't the faintest idea what any of them were going to do to stop him, but she kept running anyway, as there seemed nothing else do.

"Grrrr!" she yelled, waving her arms to distract him. The pony's ears went back even farther in alarm, but he began to veer away from this madwoman, away from the gate. "Grrrr!" He hesitated, fatally for his ambition to break his leg on the five-bar, and Alison then had him by the head, clinging onto the halter, putting all her weight into it. She was a tall, well-built woman, and Brimstone was no match for her. She pushed hard against his chest with her backside, and he subsided, chastened, against the gatepost. They both stood panting and sweating in the afternoon sun.

Laura was soon with them. Without a second thought, she whipped off her shirt and draped it across the terrified pony's eyes, effectively blinkering him.

"There, there," she soothed, stroking his neck, nuzzling his chin. "It's all right, boy, it's all right. Well done, Alison. I can't thank you enough. If he'd lamed himself for the gymkhana, we'd never have heard the end of it from Feckless. Or he could easily have broken his neck."

Alison began to laugh. There was something surreal about the sight of Laura standing there in her lacy bra and Brimstone festooned with a pink shirt with a Pony Club logo. Soon Laura joined in. "I must look bizarre. Thank God there are no fathers about."

"He just went potty." Edwina was now beside them, flushed and unnaturally garrulous. "Potty."

"It's all right, dear." Laura spoke as soothingly to her eldest daughter as she had to the frightened horse. "We saw. Aslan must have startled him, coming out of the stable like that without warning."

"He's not usually bothered by Aslan." Edwina lifted the shirt from the pony's head. "All right now, old boy? Come on, then." Her voice softened and the little horse responded gratefully, lowering his chin into her outstretched hand as though embarrassed by his recent outburst. She handed the shirt back to her mother with her free hand.

"Thank you, dear, but I think I'll put a clean one on. Perhaps you'd better worm him in the paddock after all." Laura turned back towards the house, walking half-naked but with head erect across the yard. "Alison? I think we've earned that tea."

3

You didn't see yourself as others did: as a pretty little girl with all the young girl's usual charms of short skirts and pink ribbons. You didn't see the world as others did; but as a distorted, a monstrous, place full of men who brushed up against you "by mistake" or called things after you in the street. Or just looked at you. That could be the worst, when they just looked. As if they knew that you were already soiled. Other girls could sit on their father's knee and cuddle up, could look to their mothers to protect them from predatory males. But not she, who made out for so long that she didn't know.

Nick had expected to find the wreckage of Deborah Tyson completed by the arson attack, but she was, if anything, better. She was not in bed when he called at the hospital the following morning but was sitting up in a chair in the day room in her pretty floral dressing gown and fluffy mules. Her hair had been combed and her face washed. Glimpsing her first through the picture window, he thought she looked serene. She would be discharged as soon as the consultant had done his daily round. They needed her bed.

The fire had been cathartic. The symbolic destruction of her world that her husband's crime and punishment had represented had been made real in the grime and ashes of the petrol bomb. Here was something that could be cleaned and rebuilt. Paintwork could be washed down; charred furniture could be replaced; new curtains could be bought; the insurance would pay for the carpets. If there was one thing no one could accuse Wesley Tyson of, it was being underinsured.

She laid down the glossy magazine she had been reading when Nick entered and gave him a smile of recognition. Her memory of their previous meeting was hazy, but she knew he had been kind and she had found, with some puzzlement, the food he had left her and had been sustained by it.

There was no one else in the day room, and Nick sat down on a low chair next to her and asked how she was. She told him that her throat was still a little sore, that her lungs felt as if they were filled with a viscous fluid, but that she felt a little better each day.

"Has Mr. Tyson been to see you?"

She nodded. "He came as soon as he heard. It doesn't . . . alter things."

"No."

"I shall go and stay with my parents and the children for a few days until I feel up to tackling the house. He must get help. That hasn't changed."

"Do you feel well enough to answer a few questions about the day of the attack?"

"Could you fetch me a glass of water?"

"Of course." He went to the little kitchen next door and brought back a plastic glass and a jug full of water. She poured some and took a sip.

"What do you want to know?"

"I'd like to know who came to the house that day."

"The doctor came again. He's been kind. People have been much kinder than I dared hope. The social worker came, said something about a support group for the victims of incest." She made a face. "What has that got to do with me?"

"I expect she just meant that as an example. There are all sorts of support groups these days for the families of people with problems—alcoholics, convicted criminals. It's to show you, among other things, that you're not alone, that these sort of problems are common except that people don't talk about them. Anyone else?" She thought hard. "Ordinary people. The milkman?"

"Yes! He wanted paying since I hadn't opened the door to him since . . . since Wesley was arrested."

"Door to door salesmen? Double glazing? That's always a good cover since nobody ever actually wants to buy any."

"You mean he might have come to the door, the man who did this, to—"

"See how the land lay? It's possible."

"People come," she said, "more than ever recently. Young men knock on the door almost every week, selling things from trays: soap and dishcloths and clothes pegs. Like the old-time gypsies, almost, when I was a child. They say they're unemployed or on some sort of scheme or disabled. They have cards with their photos on which they wave at you very quickly so you don't get a chance to read them. I never know what to say to them. I end up buying things I don't want at prices twice what I'd pay at the supermarket or from the catalog. I'm a bit afraid of them, I think. They can be rude if you say, 'Not today, thank you.'"

"And did any of them come that day?"

"I don't think so. Not that day. Not Wednesday." She drank some more of the water as he asked her to take him through that night step by step.

"It was hot and it took me ages to get to sleep. I just had a sheet over me, but even that felt damp and heavy. I'm not used to being alone either, not at night. But I did get off in the end, just after midnight, I heard the clock strike."

"And what's the next thing you remember?"

"I found myself dreaming that it was Guy Fawkes Night. There were me and Wesley and the children, only they were all a few years younger than they are now. So were we, me and Wesley. We were happy, all of us. About five years ago, it must have been. No, seven, because Tina was little more than a baby and Wesley built a huge bonfire in the garden and made a guy to go on top of it and said it was General Galtieri. He's very patriotic, Wesley; he always votes Conservative."

Nick let this non sequitur pass.

"We all had sparklers, all except Tina, and he let off rockets and Roman candles and I wouldn't let the boys have any bangers.

"It was a damp night but Wesley had put paraffin on the bonfire and it burned up very high after a while and the garden was getting hotter and hotter and the smoke was starting to get in my eyes and something, someone, was telling me that I must wake up and I wasn't sure that I wanted to at first but then there was shouting and hammering on the front door and I heard a window being smashed downstairs and then I really was awake and the room was full of smoke."

She began to cough as if reliving the night and Nick made her stop and poured her a fresh glass of water.

"You're doing wonderfully."

Her voice was hoarser as she resumed. "Then there was the noise of the front door being smashed in. I got up and went out onto the landing. The smoke was pouring up the stairs but they weren't really damaged and I could see the hall was full of people. Someone said to wait because the fire engine was on its way but someone else said, no, the stairs were intact, I must come down while I still could. I didn't know what to do so I just stood there and then a man came up with a wet handkerchief round his face and led me down. He risked himself to save *me*. I don't remember what happened then until I woke up here and my chest felt so sore and heavy."

She stopped, exhausted with the effort and he said, "That's marvelous, Deborah. Really marvelous," although it seemed that she had nothing new to tell him.

It wasn't until Sunday that Nick found time to go back and check up on Lucy again. Arson was one of his least favorite crimes in that it threw up, in a sense, too many clues. The Scenes of Crime Officers were at the house for days; they analyzed the type of petrol used to start the blaze and the bottle which contained it. They checked the charred door for fingerprints—round the letter box, on the knocker. The flower beds were fruitlessly checked for footprints. Nothing brought him any closer to his perpetrator.

So he was glad, late that morning, to turn his car once more along the dirt track to High Wind, and—if he were honest—to be free of his shadow again. He assumed that the mysterious Ryder Drew would be long gone, no doubt with an expensive order for a portfolio of pictures of the budding model which would never come to anything. He was surprised, then, and not displeased, to find a white BMW parked alongside Lucy's Citroen in the drive.

There was a change in Lucy that was immediately apparent: she was, quite simply, happier. She answered the front door, which was closed this time, beaming a welcome, and ushered him into the sitting room, where the hitherto faceless Drew was taking pictures of Hortense as she giggled and postured on the hearthrug in front of the inglenook.

There was something very attractive about Ryder Drew: if Nick had been a woman he would probably have fallen in love with him on the spot. But he was a man that other men took to as well. He was about thirty, tall without being offensively so, straight and muscular. He had blond hair, cropped short at present, and blue eyes which held Nick's as straight as any con man's. His clothes—white jeans, blue silk shirt—were elegant without looking as if he'd taken any trouble over them. Nick, who pulled on whatever came to hand in the morning, usually what he had pulled off the previous night, felt vaguely jealous.

He had a pleasant voice too: quiet and low, accentless. His handshake was firm without wanting to engage in an arm-wrestling contest. His hand wasn't sticky with the heat. Lucy was regarding her new acquisition, rightly, with pride. They had exchanged a few pieces of small talk by now— how glorious the weather was, how lovely the valley looked in the morning heat haze, how long Drew had been here and how long he intended to stay. It wouldn't set the Hop on fire as conversation, but anyone who said, with apparent sincerity, that he couldn't think of anywhere he would rather be on a perfect English summer's day than in the moors and valleys, coasts and cliffs around Hopbridge had no trouble stealing a corner of Nick's insular heart.

Drew was smiling a lot at Lucy, his eyes bright with something: love or desire. He looked greedy for her and Nick felt extraneous. Lucy's prediction of never feeling randy again, and of not having anyone to 'libid' with, had in a short space of time been proved spectacularly wide of the mark. He could now make out the smell of a traditional Sunday roast cooking—this was family-making with a vengeance.

Lucy eagerly produced a folder full of Hortense for his inspection: Hortense in her bath, Hortense lying naked on her back on the lawn, Hortense having her stewed apple, her little features screwed up in disdain. She drew his attention to their technical proficiency, and Ryder looked pleased and a little shy. They seemed good to Nick, and he did not hesitate to say so, while adding that he was no expert.

"I showed them to an agent I know up in The Smoke," Drew said, 'and he's definitely interested, wants to see some more. Ethnic minorities are really in at the moment. A lot of the top women models are black these days, you know. And look at her hair." He fingered it like an owner. "Like black silk. She won't even have to have it straightened."

"I should hope not!" Nick said.

"Oh, don't be so stuffy, Nick." Lucy laughed and pressed closer against Drew, who put an arm round her waist. Nick longed suddenly for her to find happiness. He wanted to tell Drew, like a heavy older brother, that he'd kill him if he did anything to hurt Lucy at this vulnerable time.

He refused their halfhearted offer that he should stay to dinner, saying truthfully that his was waiting for him at home.

■   ■   ■

Nick was eating a sandwich in his office the following Monday lunchtime. He was expecting Jim back at any moment, since the reporter had rung in first thing to say he had been delayed. So when there was a knock at the door, he assumed that Jim was back and was only surprised that he hadn't walked straight in.

"Come in!"

Bill Deacon, his regular sergeant, still convalescing from his last operation, entered the room. He was a very tall man who had once been burly but had been thinned down drastically in the course of his treatment, shedding a good five years in the process. He wore a youthful pair of jeans rather self-consciously and an open-necked shirt.

"Bill! Great to see you," Nick said. "When are you coming back?"

Bill sat down and looked gloomily round the scruffy little office where the two of them had bent their heads over so many problems together. "Not for ages, sir. That's what I've just come to tell you."

"Eh? I thought the Doc was going to sign you fit for work any day now."

"So did I. Well, this morning I went for my fortnightly checkup and he said I could start work again soon. So I said I couldn't wait to get back in CID, and he looked at me as if I was barmy and said it would be months before he could allow that. Turns out to be a desk job they've all got in mind for me. Bloody paper-pushing, starting with part-time work. And then I might have to have another operation when I'm fully recovered from the first. Meanwhile, it's the low-fat diet, no beer and lots of gentle walking."

"Oh, Bill. I am sorry."

"You don't have to say that," he said miserably. "If I was you I'd be more than happy to have a young female DS to work with instead."

"Rubbish. We're a team, you and I. It's not the same without you."

"They say she's turned out pretty good."

"She is good but that means she won't be hanging around here all that long, in this one-horse town. She'll be promoted and be off back to HQ in no time. Your job is waiting for you here, Bill, just as soon as you're well enough. Keep that in mind."

"I saw Miss Alison the other day," Bill said, making an effort to look more cheerful. "Out hacking on the moors. Lovely horsewoman, ain't she?"

"So I hear. In fact, she told me so herself so it must be true."

"Trudi, my youngest, she's got that keen on horses."

"I know. All teenage girls go through that phase, don't they?"

"Yeah, but she's extra keen. Spends every spare moment grooming and mucking out or whatever they call it. She's going in for the gymkhana on Saturday, and she really thinks she's gonna win the jumping cup, or whatever they call it, this year. Horses is all we ever hear about from her these days." Bill got up. "I'll let you get on. See you around the station, I expect."

"Pop in any time. I may need to bounce some ideas off you."

"That's Miss Walpole's job now, ideas-bouncing. Still, if you've got any little clerical jobs need doing." He looked at Nick with pathetic eagerness. "Anything useful I can do."

"Well, there is one little thing."

"Yeah?"

"Just a name through the police computer, that's all. Sorry."

"Oh." Bill took a notebook and pencil. "Who is it?"

"Ryder Drew."

"Rider?"

Nick spelled it for him.

"Well, there shouldn't be more than one of them on the computer. I'll see to it today. Give my regards to Miss Alison. See you."

He went out of the room, his shoulders drooping, his step unhurried, as if he had nowhere special to go and nothing to do when he got there.

4

"And don't forget," Alison called out as Nick left the house the next morning, "that we promised to go to that concert in Taunton tonight."

"Ugh. What is it again?"

"Mahler."

"Ugh."

"I've got the tickets. We promised. You know Marybeth is playing first violin. It's her big night, so make sure you're home by six-thirty."

"Wild horses wouldn't keep me away."

Since term had just ended, Nick thought he might occupy himself with a visit to the local primary and middle school where Felicity and Grace were pupils. He felt a moral imperative to be out doing something every hour of the day so that Jim wouldn't get bored. Accordingly, he rang the school that morning and was told that Mr. Walters, the head teacher, could see him in the afternoon.

"I'm getting some nice pictures," Jim said. He produced a print of the one he had taken of Nick at his desk. "Prezzie." Nick thought it made him look constipated but thanked Jim and slipped it into his drawer.

"I don't think you'd better take any pictures of the school or the headmaster," he said. "That might not go down too well."

"Don't pedophiles often seek out jobs that give them access to children?" Jim asked as they drove to the school. "Teaching, for example?"

"And I don't think you'd better make remarks like that to him either," Nick said firmly.

Strangely, the school seemed almost as inhabited as in term time. Bands of small boys and girls aged from about nine to twelve were weeding in the gardens, painting not-very-straight white lines on the playing field and, in the first classroom Nick looked into, feeding a growing family of gerbils.

"Can I help you, sir?" a chunky boy of about eleven, with red hair and freckles, squared up to Nick like a prize fighter—polite, while making it clear that idle spectating was not encouraged.

"I was looking for the headmaster."

"The head teacher," the boy corrected him. "I'll show you the way." He put his docile gerbil back in its cage, wiped his hands down the front of his shirt, and led them to the oldest part of the buildings—a long, low Victorian block—and flung open the first door they came to, without knocking.

"Visitors!" he yelled at the top of his voice.

Unfortunately, the head teacher was just inside the door, bending slightly over a filing cabinet, and got the full blast of this in his right ear.

"Thank you, Wayne." He rubbed the side of his head. "I may eventually regain the use of this ear."

"Sorry, Pete." Wayne laughed without contrition. Walters ruffled the boy's hair and sent him on his way with a simulated kick in the pants.

"They don't call me Pete during term time," he said, "in case you were wondering. We drop the formalities in the hols. He's a nice kid, against all the odds."

He was an undersized man of about forty—not more than five feet five inches tall and inclined to be chubby. His face was still unlined, his fine fair hair tumbled gently to his shoulders, and his blue eyes were candid and direct. He smiled as he offered them his hand as if genuinely pleased to see them. He looked a little like a large child himself. This effect was heightened by his clothes. He was wearing corduroy jeans which had been let down at the hem, as if he were still growing, and a stained tartan shirt topped by a knitted tie and a fairisle slipover.

"Not my term-time wear," he explained apologetically, "but I'm turning out files today and it can get a bit dusty. I didn't know you were coming until—"

Nick assured him that he would not be judged by his attire. He introduced Humbleby and explained his role, and Walters offered them both coffee.

"This is a hive of industry," Nick remarked, accepting a ginger biscuit.

"The cuts, you know. The PTA decided that as much of the handy work as possible should be done without recourse to expensive professionals. So we get fathers on call to come and clear blocked drains in the winter and elder brothers repainting the school hall in the evenings."

"Remarkable," Jim said. "It's all so different from the big city, isn't it?"

"And the kids wanted to do their bit, so they do the gardening and so on. It's good for them—gives them a sense of responsibility, of giving to the community as well as taking from it. I think it helps them grow up."

"And they give up their holidays?"

"We've a full house now; give it another week and they'll all be off to Penzance or Benidorm for a fortnight and the place will be like a graveyard. I shall be off myself, walking in the Lakes. Now," he leaned back in his chair and regarded them seriously, "what can I do for you gentlemen?"

Nick explained the purpose of his visit. Walters had read about the arrest of Bottone and Tyson in the local papers.

"Child pornography, yes. It's a growing problem, I believe, and a very worrying one. I have no children myself, never been married, but most of my colleagues are also parents . . . well, it's a tough business and seems to get tougher all the time and I'm often glad I've been spared. I love these kids, but I give them back at the end of the day and sleep quietly in my bed."

"Are you familiar with the danger signs of child abuse?" Nick asked.

He nodded vigorously. "Most certainly. We're very alert to the problem these days—we have to be, sadly. I went to a seminar just a couple of years ago."

Jim took out his notebook and began to make a neat list down the left-hand side of the page. He drew a very creditable straight line freehand down the center, and Nick wondered what the right-hand column was reserved for. He couldn't help thinking at times that Jim was a bit of an old woman.

Walters began to enumerate the signs that he looked for, interrupted every few minutes by the opening of the door and a shouted question or a brief, "Oh, sorry, Pete." He

147

seemed able to field these annoyances without losing his train of thought, and Nick felt like asking him what the secret was.

"We look out for any unexplained drop in performance," he was saying, "childish behavior—"

"Don't you expect childish behavior in children of that age?" Nick queried. "By definition?"

"Perhaps I should have said a reversion to more childish behavior. You might get a hitherto advanced ten-year-old suddenly trying to bring her teddy into school and talking baby talk to it—"

"Someone told me the opposite can be true, though," Nick butted in. "That the child in question may be precocious."

"Just to makes things difficult, yes. No, Micky, I don't know where Mr. Sanders is. I haven't seen him since lunchtime. Then there's things like lying and stealing. Obviously you always get a certain amount of that, and it may just be that the child has yet to learn right from wrong or is getting into bad company."

"Or it may be a cry for help?"

"Exactly. The child is told by the adult that he mustn't tell anyone about their little bedtime games, you see. If he does the adult will go to prison, okay, but the child may go into care, which the adult makes out to be a sort of prison."

"Which it is," Humbleby muttered.

"The child can't bring himself to betray the adult directly, but something like petty theft can result in an interview with, well, me, or even a child psychiatrist, and the truth may come tumbling out."

"What else?"

The door opened and a little Asian girl in a beautiful silk

sari glided silently into the room as if on castors, said, "Oh, sorry, Pete," in an unusually thick West Country burr, and glided out again.

"There's unsuitably sexual behavior—flirting, I suppose you would call it, obsession with the private parts. Or it may manifest itself as a physical complaint—headaches or upset stomachs—or the mother may report an outbreak of bed-wetting."

"Don't the mothers know what's going on?" Jim asked. He sat with his pen poised above the page, too fascinated to remember to make notes on his carefully drawn schema.

"She may not know, or she may not want to know," Nick said.

"It's not always the father that's responsible," Walters pointed out. "It may be a friend of the family or another father in the babysitting circle, in which case the mother, and the father too, may be quite oblivious."

"What about someone else in a position of trust?" Jim asked. "Youth club leaders, vicars—"

"Teachers?" Walters suggested. "Was that what you were going to say?"

"Well, yes."

"It does happen. I'd be lying if I said—can you catch me later, Kelly?—it didn't."

"What do you do if you suspect that a child is being abused?" Nick asked.

"Act as quickly as possible. Find a reason to send the child to see the school nurse, have a physical examination and a little chat. Hope you're wrong."

"And if you're not?"

"Social Services first; then maybe the police. I take the advice of Social Services on that one. It's not always in the family's best interest for the father to be taken away and locked up. If he can be made to see that what he is doing is wicked and wrong, it may be possible to salvage the family unit."

"Can I ask how many instances you've come across, personally?"

Walters considered this while indistinguishable twin boys came in to ask if he had any elastic bands, were directed wordlessly to a drawer in the corner table and left again with a boxful.

"I've been teaching in primary schools for fifteen years, been Head here for five. Maybe one case a year on average. More over the last few years, but that may just be that we've been taught to recognize the signs—it doesn't necessarily mean that it's becoming more common."

"You know Felicity Bottone, I take it?"

"Certainly. And her sister Grace. Unusually bright girls, both of them."

"What about Edwina? Was she here at some stage?"

"Who?"

"Oh, it doesn't matter." He remembered now that Edwina had been away at boarding school, unlike the other girls. No doubt following the wishes of the late, patrician Edwin Rutherford. "You haven't noticed any . . . problems?" he went on.

"Ah, I see. You think that the father may have been . . . I never met him; it was always Mrs. Bottone who came to parents evenings and so on—charming woman. I thought it was just Latin demarcation—that the children were the woman's department. Let me see. Difficult. As I say, they're very bright girls. Felicity's main problem is that she's easily bored. She finds the work her classmates do laughably easy most of the time. When children are bored they play up, are naughty, cheeky, play truant."

"She does that?"

"Occasionally."

"Has she many friends?" Nick asked.

"I think not, but she shows no sign of feeling the want of them."

"Does she get into trouble? Get punished?"

"Teachers can take a lot of cheek from children who are so obviously intelligent, I find. It's the thick ones who grind you down. Susan Mortimer! Put that back!"

"I was hopeless at school," Jim said cheerfully. "Completely hopeless. Just mucked about."

"Were you in care?" Nick asked as they drove back to the station. "I don't want to be nosy but something you said—"

"From the age of seven," Jim said. "Children's homes, short-term fostering."

"What happened when you were seven?"

"Well, let's see. My father was an alcoholic."

"Ah, I get it."

"Which is why I don't drink, as you just inferred. Mum had two more kids, couldn't cope. Wouldn't give me up for adoption, on the other hand. Just inadequate, I suppose."

Nick murmured condolences. Humbleby said that it had all been a long time ago. "Anyway, I was probably better off in care. Dad could get violent."

"Poor old Jim."

"Wish I'd been to a school like that," he said. "Where you get to keep gerbils and plant flowers and call the Head, Pete."

"I agree that it's good for the kids, gives them responsibility, confidence. You can't imagine that Wayne kid letting anyone mess him about, can you? He'd scream blue murder."

"I like kids," Jim said. "They're restful, if you see what I mean. They don't seem to expect so much from you as grown-ups do; nothing seems to surprise them. Hope you catch the bastards behind this pornography scam and make them suffer."

Bill reported back that there was no sign of Ryder Drew on the Police National Computer.

"Is that good news, or bad?" he wanted to know.

"Good. Definitely good."

Now he had to go up to the stables again and talk to Laura.

"Jim," he said, "how would you like to spend the rest of today shadowing Shirley for a change?"

"On the arson case? Fine by me."

"Only I'm calling it a day now. Alison and I have an engagement this evening."

Jim went obediently off to the incident room in search of Sergeant Walpole. As soon as he had gone, Nick contacted Dr. Brewster and asked for a good female doctor. Mike put him on to Marion Slater up the valley in Hopwood.

"Good bedside manner," he said. "Great with children. Has your Watson, your anal-retentive friend, developed my photograph yet? Helen was saying she hadn't any recent ones of me, wouldn't be able to give the police a decent description of me if I couldn't find my way home from the Eagle one day and went missing."

Nick laughed. Anally retentive was exactly what Jim was. "I'll remind him."

He rang Dr. Slater, introduced himself, and explained what he wanted. She said she was doing evening surgery that night and would wait in for him.

"Oh, dear," Nick murmured, looking at his watch. "I don't see how I'm going to be home by six-thirty." He picked up the telephone.

"You promised," Alison said when he explained.

"I didn't say 'Cross my heart and hope to die in a cellar full of rats,' though," he pointed out.

"I shall ring Davey Jones and get him to escort me," she said. "I'm sure he'll be only too delighted."

Nick gave a low whistle. "Sounds like you're in for a boring evening."

"He's very nice."

"Yeah. That's what I said."

"You'd be there fast enough if it was an Edith Piaf concert."

"So would a lot of people. She's been dead twenty-five years."

"Fuck you, Nick Trevellyan."

"I'll be home in time for that."

She snorted and hung up. He knew she must be using the cordless telephone, whose main drawback, as far as Alison was concerned, was that you couldn't slam the receiver down. He smiled to himself. He didn't have to go to the concert. Life wasn't all bad.

5

Jim was clicking away happily inside the mobile incident room. Shirley could see no reason why he shouldn't preserve the chaos for posterity.

"Have you met Mrs. Tyson, Shirley?" he asked.

"I spoke to her at the hospital but she was still very groggy then."

"Reminded me a bit of my mum—just can't cope."

"I'd be in a bit of a state if I'd just found out that my husband's tastes ran to 'chickens,'" she said, "and then been burned out of my own house."

"You'd have to know, wouldn't you? Surely there would be signs."

"Meaning that Mrs. Tyson is guilty by association?"

"Well, you know what I mean."

"No. I'm not sure I do."

Humbleby shrugged. "Is there any progress with the case?"

"The rag was an old white cotton handkerchief, the sort you get at Woolworths or any department store."

"In Agatha Christie these things have laundry marks," Jim said, as though inspired.

"You send a lot of your hankies to the laundry these days, do you, Jim?"

"Ah. It's not all progress, then, from the detective's point of view."

"I often think how nice it would be if I had a few gossipy housemaids and under-gardeners to interview. It must have been so much more difficult to keep secrets with a full staff of servants."

"I don't know how people stood it." Jim shivered. "There can't have been any privacy—bit like a children's home."

"That's good from a reporter, complaining about having your privacy invaded."

"Now, now. I was going to ask, actually, if I could do an in-depth personal interview with you. Your views on women in the police force, how it affects your private life, stuff like that."

"I'm not sure."

"You'd take a lovely photo, pretty girl like you." Shirley was flattered, despite herself. "Maybe I could talk to your boyfriend—"

"I haven't got a boyfriend."

"Hard, is it? Being a policewoman?"

"At times."

"I can bring that out in my article. The prejudice, the machismo, everything that militates against women in the force."

"Militates."

"Militates. That's what I said."

"I'll think about it. I'd have to get it cleared with the chief inspector."

"What does a woman detective sergeant do with her free time, then?"

"This WDS goes to films—"

"How about we take in a film some time, you and me?"

155

"I, um, I'll have to think about it, Jim."

"Fair enough."

"I also spend a lot of time practicing my judo."

"Blimey!" Jim looked suitably cowed. "So," he went on, "where do we go from here?"

"*We* carry on taking statements."

"All by yourself?"

"I'm heavily reliant on uniformed at the moment with two DCs away."

"Your Mr. Burcombe?"

"Our Mr. Burcombe, as you say."

She had to admit that this was one thing Colin Burcombe was good at: the little, painstaking checks that drove you mad. He was asking at every garage in the valley about petrol purchased in the can, even though, as he pointed out, it was more likely to have been siphoned out of a tank. He had got half his uniformed relief organized on a systematic house-to-house inquiry radiating out from Dove Crescent and Bridgwater Drive. He was checking up on them himself and could often winkle more information out of reluctant witnesses with his abrupt manner than any amount of Shirley's playing-it-by-the-book.

"This is a built-up residential area," he had said. "The fire broke out at about one o'clock in the morning. It was a hot night. Someone locally must have still been awake, going to get a glass of water, must have seen the arsonist in the telephone box or actually at the house. Stands to reason."

"The trouble is," Shirley had pointed out, "a lot of them don't want to help. They think Tyson has just got what was coming to him, and Mrs. Tyson too."

"Then they must be made to see things differently, Shirlgirl." He had smiled his sharp-toothed smile at her. "And do their bloody civic duty."

He had been as good as his word.

"Come on, love. Don't give me that 'Can't remember which night it was' rubbish. It was only a couple of days ago. Switch your brain on. It was Wednesday. You got home from work. You made the beans on toast or the egg and chips. You watched *Coronation Street* and *The Sting*— wished your old man looked a bit more like Robert Redford. It finished at midnight. You made yourself some cocoa. Remember now?

"It was a hot night. You couldn't get comfy. The old man was a bit the worse for wear when he got back at closing time. You can see that phone box on the corner from your bedroom window—look at it, all lit up. So, who was in there that night? Round one o'clock? Think!"

It was past six o'clock by the time Nick reached the stables. He went in at the back door and seated himself at Laura's long kitchen table like the old friend he already felt himself to be. Apart from Laura, only Felicity was there, hunched up at the head of the table drinking a glass of milk and reading a Penguin Classic.

"Hello, Uncle Nick."

"What are you reading, Felicity?"

She didn't turn the book up for his inspection as people usually did when asked this question, but said, *"Great Expectations"* without looking up. She turned over another page. Nick was impressed. He'd still been working his way through The Famous Five at the age of nine. He had a vivid memory, too, of being terrified by the Wicked Queen in

Snow White at that age, never mind Miss Havisham.

"She's read more books than Roald Dahl's Matilda," Laura said, putting a mug of frothy coffee down in front of him. "She graduated from children's books a couple of years ago. Run out now and get some fresh air, Feckless."

She sat down herself. Felicity looked up a little sulkily, and Laura jerked her head towards the door in a commanding gesture. "Go and help Edwina groom Abelard—I noticed earlier that he'd managed to get dirt all over his withers and Alison wants to take him out for a hack tomorrow."

"If you mean you want to talk to Uncle Nick in private, why don't you just say so?" Felicity folded down the top left-hand corner of her book to mark her page and placed it on the sideboard before walking out into the yard.

"My father is dead," she called over her shoulder, "and nobody gives a damn."

"I give a damn," Nick said.

Laura sat down next to him. For once she was not in riding clothes and wore a white cotton dress circled with a red belt which showed off her tiny waist. She looked young and pretty; she must have been like a fairy too, he thought, twenty-five, thirty years ago.

He had stopped to admire some of the horses on his way in. With the invention of the internal combustion engine he had assumed horses to be superfluous to human requirements and kept merely for show, but watching Edwina floating round the paddock bareback like a sadly over-dressed Godiva, he was undergoing a change of heart. They were always much bigger than you remembered them as being, and there was something hugely erotic about a woman on horseback, the pair moving together with grace and strength. No wonder people said horses were a sexual substitute for adolescent girls.

"Which one is Abelard?" he asked, wanting to picture Alison mounted.

"The chestnut gelding with the blaze and one white sock." Nick opened his mouth again."Which is to say gingery-red—lighter than a bay—with a white stripe down his face and a white patch above one of his hooves. And before you ask me why we don't just call them light and dark brown and why we call white horses, gray—I don't know, nor does anyone else."

"So little Brimstone's technically gray, is he?" Nick felt he was overloading on equine information.

"Correct. Only Lipizzaners are called white."

"What? Those Viennese ballet dancers?"

She laughed. "I don't much like watching horses do all that dressage either," she admitted, "it's not natural. Give me a good jumper or a good hunter any day."

Nick could hear Felicity calling out to her older half-sister in the stable yard, and he recalled the reason for his visit. "I suppose she does pretty well at school, Felicity, being so bright?"

"Not as well as she should, really. She doesn't try. The other kids in her class are too slow for her so she just plays up a lot of the time, cheeks the teachers. They don't like her much. Nor do the other kids."

"I like her," Nick said.

"Good. So do I."

"But the school tells me she plays truant quite a lot."

Laura spread her hands helplessly. "I send her every morning, give her her packed lunch. I drive her down to the bottom of the hill with Grace to catch the school bus,

watch them get on it. But she doesn't take orders from anyone."

"So she's a bit of a loner?

Laura nodded.

"Would you say that she has behavioral problems?"

Laura sighed. "I knew we'd get to that before long.
Look, Nick, Arturo wasn't a pedophile, okay? He was just
a supplier, a middleman, trading on other people's weak-
nesses."

"People who peddle that sort of thing are usually con-
sumers too, you know. You don't find many drug pushers
who haven't got a habit."

"Arturo was quite normal sexually. Believe me."

"I expect Mrs. Tyson thought the same thing about her
husband."

"It beats me. How could you not know a thing like that
about your own husband, for God's sake? And yet, I don't
know, when you look around you and see couples who
barely communicate, perhaps I'm stupid and naive to be
surprised."

"They're such lovely kids too."

"My lot? Yes, I suppose they are."

"It's just that abused children are often precocious, old
for their years, don't get on with other kids, skip school."

"Just like Feckless?"

"Would it worry you very much for her to have a quiet
word with a very nice doctor, a woman doctor, a little examination. Nothing to frighten her."

"If you must."

"Thanks."

"I don't suppose you really need my permission, do you,
Chief Inspector?"

She raised her head and looked him straight in the eye,

her loose blonde hair flicking back from her face. Her anger was vibrant. There was a challenge in the air; something very like electricity crackled between them. He wanted to take hold of her and reassure her, but she might give him a 240-volt shock. It disturbed him, as if he had just been unfaithful.

"That's just the sort of reaction I wanted to avoid by asking for it," he said, after a pause in which he collected himself.

She subsided. The gauntlet was withdrawn. "Sorry. I was out of order."

"I'm asking partly because I consider you a friend and partly because I probably do need it, actually. Arturo is dead: we're not going to be charging him with anything. I've no proof he was involved in producing as well as distributing the stuff. I'd be hard pushed to get an examination done on such a young child without your consent."

"I already said, yes. If we're friends, I don't want you going through the rest of your life suspecting me of hiding something and lying to you."

"You put it very harshly."

"I'm a realist."

Nick, wanting to win back her confidence, began to explain. "The thing is, you see, that I don't know where a lot of the photos come from. Films and magazines, okay, they come from abroad—Germany, Denmark, the States. Most of them are years old, too. But there were some still photos that looked quite recent, and I want to know where they came from."

"Didn't they include faces?" she was asking, spared, unlike him, the memories. "So you could see they're not my kids?"

"No, and that's quite unusual too; they normally like to

161

include faces so the customer can be sure that the kid is as young as she—or he—is cracked up to be." Laura grimaced. "I think they were amateur," he went on, "like most child porn. I think they originated in this country, in this region, although don't ask me why. That's part of the problem. I haven't a shred of proof for any of what I suspect."

"Tell me something, Nick. . . . Aren't you afraid of being corrupted by your job, by all the sickening things you have to look at and hear?"

Nick did not reply, did not tell her that there were times when he felt both tarnished and afraid.

"I suppose someone has to do it," she said eventually, "and I'd rather it was you than most other policemen I've ever met, than your Mr. Burcombe, say. I wouldn't put it past Arturo to be involved in production either, but not with his own kids. Never that."

Nick shook his head sadly. "That's what everyone thinks, that the kids used in these films and magazines are runaways or kidnap victims. The horrible truth is that they're usually the photographer's own children or step children or children 'rented' to him by their parents by the hour."

"Shit!" Laura picked up a half-empty bottle of wine from the table, uncorked it, poured herself a glass, and drained half of it off. She offered the bottle to Nick, who shook his head. "Yes, it's a bit early for me, too, but—" He remembered suddenly how much she had suffered.

"You don't think Arturo committed suicide, do you, Nick? Be honest with me."

"You're right: I don't think so. I think he was killed by one of his suppliers or one of his customers to stop him naming names. But no one believes me: no one chooses to believe me."

"Which is why you come to see me in the evenings and at weekends? It's your own little project?"

He hesitated then said, "Let's say I have plenty to keep me busy during normal working hours."

"Arturo is dead, Nick. He was not a good man, but let him rest in peace. Let me bury him and get on with my life. Leave it. Please. For my sake and that of my children."

"I can't just close my eyes, my dear. It's not me."

Laura got up and leaned heavily over the bottom half of the kitchen door.

"'If it were done, when tis done,'" she said, "'then t'were well it were done quickly.' Feckless! Here a minute. Uncle Nick wants a word with you."

Felicity climbed into the back of Nick's Peugeot five minutes later. She seemed pleased at the prospect of an outing. Laura had added a thin scarlet jacket to her attire and, as he leaned across to belt her into the front passenger seat, he could feel the warmth of her still body through it. She closed her eyes as he started the engine and began to pull out of the yard.

"I'm not a very good passenger," she said.

"That's all right," Nick replied. "I'm not a very good driver."

6

"So that's a weight off my mind," Nick said later. It was after midnight by the time Alison got back from the concert,
and he was making hot chocolate for them both, stirring
the mixture hard with a great rattling of spoons.

"You didn't really think Felicity was being abused, did
you?" she asked. "She's not one of nature's victims—anyone can see that."

"I think you forget how young she is; it's easily done
since she seems so mature. But Dr. Slater was marvelous—
very gentle and tactful—and she's adamant that Felicity is
virgo intacta and shows no other signs of abuse."

"A relief, as you say." Alison seemed a little abstracted
that evening. "So what now?"

"There's a man on my books who's done time for molesting children in the past. He's been out for a while and is
no longer on parole and seems to have no fixed abode. So I
think I'll take a run out tomorrow morning. I think I know
someone who might know where I can find him."

"A couple of witnesses have mentioned a van," Shirley
said.

"A van?"

"Parked by the call box. It may have been orange and it may have had some kind of white markings on it."

"A lot of vans are *red,*" Jim said.

"Orange was what one witness said. He was definite."

"And a lot of delivery vans have white markings, birds in flight, arrows, anything to signify speed." Nick was thoughtful. "Any vestige of a number?" She shook her head. "Not even if it was A-reg or X-reg or whatever? Okay, just add the info to the rest of the profile we're building up."

"It's something, a van."

"It's something and nothing."

"Better than a car," Jim said, correctly.

"Well. I'm out on the road, probably for the rest of the day." Nick got up and jingled his car keys in his pocket. "Bleep if you need me. Come along, Jim."

"Woof, woof." Humbleby did an impression of a dog coming to heel.

It was the fifth pub they had tried—the White Horse, in Gladstone Road—and Nick spotted her at once in the almost-empty public bar: a ragbag of a woman who might have been any age from thirty to sixty. No, maybe not thirty.

"Look, Jim," he said in a low voice, "would you do me a big favor and wait in the car. I shan't be long."

"Why?"

"Because some of the people I have to talk to are nervous types. It's hard to win their confidence and get anything out of them. I'll get on better on my own."

"All right." Jim turned away reluctantly. "But you'll tell me what you've learned after?"

"I promise."

Jim went more willingly, and Nick walked across the empty public bar and stopped at her table. "May I buy you a drink?" She glanced up, then gave him a longer, appraising, look. She offered him no sign of recognition.

"If you like, love."

"What'll it be? Gin?"

She looked at her empty beer glass and said, "If you're buying, love."

"Anything with it?"

"No ta."

Nick fetched her a large gin and a jug of water and sat down next to her on the bench. It was eleven in the morning, and she was already three-quarters drunk. She smelled very faintly: a mixture of beer, sweat, unwashed clothing, and cologne. She added a few droplets of water to the gin, took a large mouthful, and became suddenly businesslike.

"What is it you're after, love? I don't do nothing kinky."

"I just want to ask you a few questions."

She put her glass down abruptly. "My God! You're the Old Bill. You nearly slipped past me. I can usually smell 'em a mile off. I must be getting old."

"I'll pay for your time."

"What's your name, love?"

"Nick."

"Mine's Ianthe."

"That's a pretty name," Nick said, meaning it. He knew perfectly well what her name was, had held many similar conversations with her over the years.

"It's my right name, too," she said. My mum got it out of

a book." She closed her eyes to prop up her failing memory and, to Nick's astonishment, began to recite.

> *From you, Ianthe, little troubles pass*
> *Like little ripples down a sunny river;*
> *Your pleasures spring like daisies in the grass,*
> *Cut down, and up again as blithe as ever.*

"She was a great reader, my mum, in between her gentlemen." She paused and took another large swig of gin, emptying the glass. "Sometimes during. Don't really rhyme though, do it—'river' and 'ever'? Bit of a cheat, if you ask me."

Nick smiled. "Your mother was in the business too?"

"Oh yes, dear."

"Want another?"

"Please."

He refilled her glass. The barman winked at him and whispered, "She's been retired for years, but she won't lie down. Or rather she will, if you see what I mean."

Nick sat down again and took a sip of his own low-alcohol lager. "I want to know about a man called Norman who used to run some girls round here."

"Norman Crick. Long, long time ago, love."

"I know. Ten years?"

"More. He went away for interfering with little boys." She made a retching noise in her throat. "I can't stand that sort of thing."

"I'm told he's back now."

"I know. I seen him."

"Recently?"

She shrugged. "Today, yesterday, last week, last month.

What's the odds? You're a nice-looking boy, dear."

"Thank you. Do you know where he's staying?"

"Glebe Street, Hopcliff," she said unexpectedly. "With a slag called Martha Greene. Fifth house along on the right." Nick tried to hide his surprise. "I'm not quite gone yet, love," Ianthe said. "He's sponged off Martha all his life and he ain't gonna stop now. What's the pig done? More of the same?"

"I don't know. That's what I want to find out."

"You're a nice-looking boy," she said again. "Want a freebie?"

"No. Thank you."

"Absolutely free and for nothing. No charge. Your lot usually do."

"Thank you. No."

"I'm perfectly clean. I make my gentlemen use rubbers. None of these diseases. Ask anyone."

"I appreciate the thought, but no."

"Don't you like women, dear?"

"I like most women and I love just one."

"Married?"

"No." Nick hesitated. "Cohabiting."

"Oh." She looked thoughtful. "I'm wasting my time, then. I mean, when a bloke's married, it's because he's too lazy to get out of it, often as not, but when he's . . . *cohabitating* . . . he's there because he wants to be. Stands to reason."

"Yes. "Nick smiled.

"Lucky girl."

"You must tell her so if you see her, Ianthe."

"Give us a kiss, then, and I'll be off on my rounds. No charge for the info." She looked at him unsteadily, a little remembrance and comprehension dawning. "Next time maybe?"

He took a five-pound note from the breast pocket of his shirt and pressed it into her hand. "No. Take it," he said as she pushed it away, and she sighed and folded it up small and tucked it down the front of her blouse. He leaned forward and kissed her lightly on the cheek.

"I'll see you again, Ianthe. Good luck."

"Too late for that, dearie."

"So are we going to talk to this Crick?" Jim asked.

"I'm going to get a search warrant first. That way I can find out if he's got any illegal magazines without giving him time to hide them."

"Is it likely he was one of Bottone's customers?"

"Let's just say that the recidivism rate is high among child molesters. They don't give them any help inside, you see. Just lock them up for the requisite number of years, often in solitary, then let them out again."

"It doesn't make sense," Jim said.

"Perhaps you should write about it."

"Perhaps I will."

It happened first when you were seven, when she was out shopping, her favorite treat. He was home to take care of you and she could go out and not worry. She could have lunch out, too, enjoy herself; he would get them something simple.

You were in your bedroom struggling with a school book. You heard him come up the stairs on padding, slippered feet, pause outside your door, open it. You turned and smiled at him. Why shouldn't you? He was your father, wasn't he? He asked what you were doing, came and put his arm round your shoulders, pretending to read the child's simple spelling book with its garish pictures.

He began to tickle you, which he knew you hated. You were squealing, squirming to get away. You flung away from him, giggling, across the narrow bed. It was early summer and you weren't wearing much—a skirt, a cotton T-shirt. He chased you; it was a game. His hand was up your skirt, as though by accident. You were pinned down across the bed now, still giggling.

But then you got frightened and told him to stop and he said that if you would just relax it would be all right. He said that it was just a game, a secret game. It was a game he played with your mother; didn't you love your mother, admire her, want to be like her? Well, then. You were too shocked and frightened to call out and there was no one to hear you if you did, no one to come to your rescue.

He put his hand over your mouth. You bit it and he slapped you, quite hard, loosening a milk tooth. His large hairy hand squeezed over your nose as well as your mouth and you thought he was going to kill you, you almost wished he would. Then you bolted to the bathroom and locked the door, bent your head over the washbasin wanting to be sick but not achieving it. He was banging on the door, demanding you unlock it. Then there was silence for a few minutes and you realized he had gone away. Then he came back, calling out in his normal friendly voice that lunch would soon be ready, nothing elaborate, just beans on toast.

You could not stay in the bathroom for the rest of your life. You could not tell your mother; it would have killed her, as he explained. Also, she would be jealous. It was your secret, yours and his. You were Daddy's little girl. He bought you sweets and comics and anything else you asked for. Your mother scolded or laughed indulgently and said he spoiled you.

The tooth fairy brought you fifty pence for your milk tooth that night

It was your fault, anyway. It didn't happen to other, normal, girls. None of the girls at school said it had happened to her. You led him on—he said so—with your short school gymslips and your white bare arms. Or else it was normal, like with all the other little girls in the pictures he showed you: girls of all races and colors, from all over the world, all loving their daddies, showing that love in the best way they knew how.

At night, in the small hours, you remembered and were afraid.

7

"Mrs. Greene?"

Nick produced his warrant card. The slatternly looking woman at the door sighed. This was apparently not a new experience for her. She could not even summon up anger, merely resignation. She was not more than forty, but she was stout and unkempt, and her hair, which had once been auburn, hung in dirty tails around her shoulders.

"I thought you was the man from the catalog. With my delivery. They get later all the time. I bin waiting—"

"I'm looking for Norman Crick," Nick interrupted. "I believe he lives here."

"I dunno about lives. He's staying here. Norm!" The woman bellowed back into the house. "For you. Police."

"Not so bloody loud, woman." The man emerged from the darkness of the hallway and said with the automatic response of his kind, "I ain't done nothing."

"I have a warrant to search these premises." He set one foot across the threshold. The small house smelt stale and poor.

"It's all right, Mum. Let me deal with this." Nick peered into the shadows to make out the new speaker.

"Blimey!" Jim said, gaping over Nick's shoulder. "It's the ginger kid from the school."

"Wayne, isn't it?" Nick said, recognizing his escort of the previous day. He was as surprised as Jim but better used to concealing it.

"I'm Wayne Greene. You'd better come in. Mum, go and make us some tea." Martha Greene wandered obediently off in the direction of the kitchen, and Wayne opened the door of the front downstairs room and said, "Would you like to come in here, sir?"

"Actually," Nick said, "I think we'll all stay together until I've carried out my search." He followed Mrs. Greene into the kitchen, almost pushing Crick along in front of him. "Now if you wouldn't mind staying in this room with my colleague, perhaps Wayne can show me over the rest of the house."

Martha Greene filled the kettle without comment. The room was not clean. Martha, the good housekeeper; if only people would live up to their names.

"Can I see the warrant?" Wayne asked. Since he was easily the most adult person in the family, Nick handed it to him. He read it and handed it back. "Let's go. Where do you want to start?"

"Upstairs."

Wayne led the way up the narrow staircase. There were three doors leading off the landing, all of them closed.

"Bathroom." Wayne pushed open the door straight ahead. "Mum's room." Another door opened. "My room at the back." There was now a lot more light on the landing and Nick could see the boy's face clearly. He looked ashamed but defiant. "I can take care of myself," he said. "And her."

"I'm sure."

"I don't need your pity."

"No. Nobody does, apparently. How old are you, Wayne?"

"Twelve." There were plenty of twelve-year-olds, he

knew, who took responsibility for ineffectual parents.

"Where does Crick sleep?" The boy pointed silently to the front bedroom. "Been here long?"

"Too long. About six weeks."

"You don't like him?"

"He's a sponger. It's not as if she's got that much for him to sponge. But what there is, he'll have." He looked hopeful. "Any chance of you taking him away?"

"That depends if I find what I'm looking for."

"Not much chance then. Nothing goes on here that I don't know about."

Nick searched the rooms while Wayne looked on in silence. It didn't take very long. He found a pile of old girlie magazines in a wardrobe in the front bedroom, but they were the kind that could be picked up at any newsagents.

"My dad's," Wayne commented. "God! They must be old."

The attic was accessible via a chest of drawers on the landing. Wayne showed him how to swing himself up. "I can get up here," he explained with a grin, "but Mum won't try and Cricky can't make it, not with his dicky lungs, so I get the place to myself. Sometimes I just sit quietly up here with the light off, and they don't know I'm in."

Nick was sorry to intrude on Wayne's private world; he could see that the boy would need a bolt-hole. Wayne grinned as Nick climbed carefully down again. "You're covered in cobwebs." He brushed him down with his hands.

"Thanks." He searched downstairs next. He could hear Crick coughing in the kitchen and Jim's low, slightly monotonous voice, droning on about something. Finally he joined them. Jim looked up at him expectantly.

"Nothing," he said.

"I told you," Crick said.

Nick was sarcastic; he didn't like having his time wasted, and this little house depressed him. "Well, I'll just have to take your word for it next time. Save myself the trouble. Come on."

"Come on what?"

"I want a word. We'll go outside to my car. It's stuffy in here."

"You just said you didn't find nothing."

"I still want a word. Come on. Come on, Jim. Thank you, Wayne."

Crick followed them, grumbling, across the road and climbed into the front passenger seat of Nick's car. He was a shabby man who was, according to his record, forty-eight but looked older. He ran his hand nervously through thinning hair. "Don't know you, do I?" he said, squinting in the light.

"I came since you've been away. I wanted to talk about your record—"

"I'm out now. Done my time! Most of it in solitary on bloody Rule forty-three." The indignation turned into an unpleasant wheezing, and color flooded into his cheeks and neck. "Emphysema," he gasped. He pulled an inhaler out of his pocket, shook it hard, breathed out to the limit of his lungs, and inhaled a burst of the chemical. A curl of blue smoke issued from his lips like Puff the Magic Dragon. He repeated the actions and put the inhaler away. He was still panting slightly, but the dangerously high color in his face began to die down. "That's better."

"But you've done time for child abuse," Nick said.

"Weren't much. Bit of flashing, bit of touching. Nothing else. The kids, they encourage you. Ask you for money. 'Quid for a feel, mister.' Then it's 'Give us a fiver or we'll tell the cops.' I can't help it. That's what the quacks say. It's not my fault."

"Do you know a man called Arturo Bottone?"

"Eh? What sort of a name's that? Never heard of him."

"Where were you on the night of July the fourth?"

"When was that?"

"A couple of weeks ago," Nick said patiently. "A Tuesday."

Crick thought about it. "In hospital," he said triumphantly. "With me emphysema."

"So whatever else Crick may have been up to, he wasn't out hanging Bottone on the night of July the fourth," Nick said later that day. "He was safely tucked up in a hospital bed with the night nurse on duty."

The hospital had confirmed that Crick had had a bad attack of asthma—a secondary symptom of his emphysema—just after lunch that day. It had been beyond the scope of his inhaler. He had been scarcely able to breathe and had been whisked off to hospital in an ambulance and kept in overnight for observation.

"As alibis go, it's good," Nick said.

"I wonder what brought the attack on, though," Jim said. "These things are often stress related. Might it have been reading about Bottone's arrest in the paper that morning?"

"You know, Jim, we'll make a detective of you yet."

"Thank you, kind sir. We're gonna keep an eye on him then?"

"We are. That kid Wayne . . . God! It makes me so angry. If that bastard lays a finger on him—"

"Wayne can take care of himself. Just like you said yesterday."

"I feel I ought to do something about him though."

"Like what? Have him taken into care? Believe me, he's

better off at home. He's obviously adequately fed and decently clothed. He won't thank you for interfering. Besides, his mum needs him."

"I expect you're right. He seems to be surviving very well."

Nick got home at about six and found Alison hard at work at her terminal in the workshop.

"You're early," she said rather coolly. "Going out again, I suppose."

"Not tonight." He sat down beside her and laid his head on her shoulder. "I'm all yours."

"In that case I'll call it a day." She was not one to bear a grudge and forgave his recent neglect of her in an instant. She stored what she was doing and switched the terminal off. She stood up and Nick rose, too, and put his arms round her.

"I love you, Alison." He stroked her cheek where her freckles had become so numerous as almost to merge in a single mass.

"I love you," she echoed. They embraced for a moment in the cool of the air-conditioned workshop.

"I do believe you do," he said.

"I just said so, didn't I?"

"Because if you didn't, you wouldn't be *cohabitating* with me, would you?"

"Have you been drinking?" She asked in amazement. He laughed and shook his head.

"I wouldn't say no to a glass of wine, though. It's my turn to cook supper, isn't it?"

"It's been your turn to cook supper for the past few days," she pointed out, "but you prefer chasing wild Italian geese."

"Name any dish from my modest repertoire and it's yours."

"How about some chicken with lemon and rosemary sauce?"

"Good choice. Go and pick me some sprigs of rosemary—for remembrance."

"Are you quite sure you haven't been drinking?"

"Quite sure." He buried his head in her hair and inhaled deeply. "You, and you alone, intoxicate me."

"You're behaving very oddly," grumbled Alison, who didn't approve of odd behavior, "and you're filthy!" She drew away from him. "You're covered in dust and there's a piece of cobweb in your hair."

"Attics are dusty."

"Well . . . what were you doing in an attic?"

He didn't answer. Instead he said, "I kissed another woman today, Alison."

She frowned.

"A woman called Ianthe."

"Nice name," she said cautiously. "Any particular reason?"

"Because she reminded me that you love me."

"I don't even know the woman, do I?"

"She's a semiretired whore, working the pubs up in West Hopbridge. A fairly regular informant. I had a drink with her at the White Horse."

". . . No, I don't think I've had the pleasure."

"Nor have I although she did offer." He laughed at her expression. "Never mind. Go forth, wench, and gather rosemary and parsley."

"Anyway," she remarked, as she left the room. "I'd have said you were cohabitating"—she clicked her tongue in exasperation—"I mean, cohabiting with me, not vice versa."

8

"There's this world," he said after dinner. He waved his hand to encompass Hope Cottage with its thick soft carpets, its welcoming lights, its comfortable sofas, its gardens and wood and paddock. And also, perhaps, Colt's Head with its rosettes and trophies, its well-groomed horses and gleaming tack. "Our world, where there are books and hot baths and clean clothes and good dinners—"

"You're over-tired," Alison said.

"Where people are decent. Not perfect: they may tell a few white lies and break the speed limit and cheat on their taxes, but they don't kill, or rape small children. They bring their kids up as best they can and try to be honest and reliable.

"Then there's the other world, the submerged tenth: Ianthe—a worn-out whore with nothing but alcohol and dreams to live on; Crick, who'll be in and out of prison until his emphysema finally releases him; Mrs. Tyson, who's been half way to madness and back again; and Wayne, who ought by rights to be a truant and a petty criminal already—"

"There you are then. Wayne is getting by, against all the odds."

"Sometimes I think I spend too much time in that other world," he muttered.

"Would you rather take a job in an office and pretend that world doesn't exist, as so many people do?"

"Some days. What do you think?"

"I think," she said gently, "that I shall run you a bath and then we shall go to bed."

Sometimes he would do it in public, taking delight in the risk. You would be sent out for a walk with him, reluctantly dragging your heels, saying you thought you had a cold coming and being told to hurry up and get your coat and not be such a baby, that not many girls got so much time and attention from papa.

So he would sit you on a stile, perhaps a mile from home, putting his arm round you, his left hand pointing out some handsome landmark while his right fingers unfastened your jeans and slid down into your panties. Once an old couple with a dog appeared from nowhere and he didn't move. They called out a cheery Good Morning and he answered them blithely. They noticed nothing. "What a dear little girl," one of them said. "You must be so proud of her."

He could touch you there but he couldn't touch your mind; that was safe from him.

The dog had growled.

It was again in the early hours of the morning that the news came through that Martha Greene's little house had gone up in flames. Nick drove the few miles to Hopcliff in record time.

Glebe Street was alive with people, looking other-worldly in the harsh red glare of the fire. In their night clothes, with pullovers hastily dragged on top and feet thrust into the nearest shoes, they might have been goblins or trolls. A uniformed constable moved to stop him as he turned into the street, then recognized the car and waved him on. Flames were shooting out of the roof of number fifteen, where Martha lived. Nick drew up at the end of the street.

"Same method," Shirley said, wrenching open the door of his car before he had even stopped. "Petrol-soaked rag through the letter box, burning spill after it. They're having more trouble putting it out this time. The houses are more cramped and more crowded. We've had to evacuate the whole street."

Nick got out. "What about the people inside?" As he spoke he could see Martha Greene standing helplessly on the pavement watching her home, and everything she owned in the world, burn.

"A man there was taken to hospital suffering from an asthma attack," Shirley was saying, "brought on more by panic than anything, I think. They had him on a ventilator. He didn't look good."

"Wayne!" Nick grabbed her by the arms and almost shook her. "Where's Wayne?"

"Who?" Shirley looked baffled, and he remembered that it had been Jim with him on his recent inquiries, that Shirley didn't know this family, had no idea what he was talking about. He released her abruptly and sprinted up the road.

"Mrs. Greene." He spun her round and she got the same treatment as Shirley. "Where's Wayne?"

She stared at him groggily, and he realized that she was—perhaps predictably—a woman who doped herself up with sleeping tablets at night. "He went up to the attic after his tea," she said finally. "Sometimes he falls asleep up there."

Wayne!

Nick ran across to the fire engine. "There may be a boy in there. In the attic."

"If there is," the Chief Fire Officer stared up at the burning shell of the roof, "he's had it."

"There must be something you can do," Nick yelled above the noise both of the conflagration and the attempts to quell it.

"None of my men are going in there at present. It would be suicide."

Nick slumped against the side of the fire engine. Smoke was getting in his eyes and making them water. His instinct had been to do something, to call Social Services, to say that Mrs. Greene wasn't fit to look after her son, to get him removed to a place of safety. But he hadn't done it; Jim had talked him out of it, convinced him to mind his own business. No, that wasn't fair; he had talked himself out of it, and now the boy—that bright little ginger-haired boy—was dead and not such a survivor after all.

The heat was palpable. People milled about in an amorphous, sulfurous haze. Surely Hell must be something like this. He felt himself swaying slightly.

"You all right, mate?" Nick was surprised to find Colin Burcombe, the uniformed Inspector, his old enemy, at his side, looking almost concerned.

"What are you doing here?" he gasped out.

"I was in the area when the call came through, picked it up on my car radio, thought I'd see if there was anything I could do." He puffed out his cheeks in a pantomime of discomfort. "It's a bit hot here, I should come away if I was you. Keep out of their way. We'll get our turn soon enough." He took Nick by the arm to preclude further argument and led him up the road to where Glebe Street intersected with Cliff Walk and some cooling breezes were sweeping in from the bay.

"Siddown," Burcombe said roughly. He spread his jacket on the pavement and Nick sat down on it. Burcombe squatted on his heels beside him and looked at him narrowly. "That smoke don't half get in your eyes—makes you look as if you're bloody crying." He took out a cigarette and lit it, fanned himself with his other hand. "As if it wasn't hot enough already. Smoke?" Nick shook his head.

"They're getting it under control," Burcombe remarked a few minutes later. "That's three houses gone beyond repair, though, I'd say. Just as well. They're no better than bloody slums, these places. No proper fireproof doors, nothing."

The firemen would be going in soon, Nick knew, taking care on the burned floorboards, since they were all big men, had to be, had to be able to carry a twelve-stone man to safety. Wayne's body wouldn't weigh half that.

"This arson's following me about," he said.

"Jee-sus!" said a voice coming up Cliff Walk behind him. It was the squeaky exhalation of a voice not quite ready to break. It was at once excited and appalled. It was also familiar. Nick spun round.

"Don't go any closer, sonny," Burcombe said, stepping forward and catching the boy by the arm. "There's nothing much to see."

"But it's my place," he said. Then again, "Jee-sus!"

"Wayne!"

Nick jumped to his feet and stared at the boy, who was fully dressed in jeans and a sweatshirt with "Pet Shop Boys" printed across it. It seemed unsuitable attire for a ghost. He was carrying a kite—a blue and yellow butterfly. "We thought you were in there. Your mum said you'd gone up to your attic and not come down."

The boy looked sheepish. "That's all she knows. I often go for a wander along the cliff at night. Once she's taken her pills, she's dead to the world. Here!" A thought struck him. "Is she all right?" Nick reassured him and pointed along the pavement to where his mother still stood for all the world like a disinterested observer.

"Oh good." He made no move to join her. "What about old Cricky?"

"Had an asthma attack. He's gone to hospital."

"He'll be all right," Wayne said with the callousness of the young. "His sort are indestructible." He held up his kite for inspection. "My birthday present arrived today. On the delivery from the catalog. I wanted to try it out on the cliff. The winds are better at night."

"Oh, Wayne!"

Nick could contain himself no longer. To the boy's considerable surprise, he grabbed him in his arms and hugged him. Burcombe stared in disbelief.

That damn smoke seemed to be getting in Nick's eyes again.

"You'll bust my kite," Wayne complained.

"I'll buy you a new one. I'll buy you two."

"The Council'll have to rehouse us now," Wayne said happily to Burcombe over Nick's shoulder.

Part Three

And I looked, and behold a pale horse and the rider's name was Death.

Revelation 6:8

1

When Bill Deacon came into Nick's office again late on Thursday afternoon, he had regained some of his old enthusiasm and launched in without preliminaries. "Look, you remember that name you asked me to run through the computer on Monday?"

"Ryder Drew, sure. You said you couldn't find anything."

"I couldn't. But things have been a bit quiet lately—all this bloody desk work—so I was amusing myself running a few permutations through."

"Oh, yes?" Nick was suddenly alert.

"I got something under Andrew Ryder."

Nick looked at him with respect. "Well done, Bill."

"Andrew Paul Ryder. One little conviction for fraud about four years ago. Up in London."

"Not exactly Jack the Ripper, is he?" Nick said, disappointed.

"So I rang the station that dealt with it and spoke to the Detective Inspector there. He knows your Mr. Ryder very well indeed. In fact he'd been wondering where he'd got to lately."

"Ah." Nick sat back in his chair, strangely pleased. There

were many men well known to the police as criminals but just too slippery ever to have anything brought home to them. If the police up in London had started keeping an eye on Ryder, that explained why he had migrated south for the summer.

"He's your basic con man," Bill was saying. "Preys on wealthy older women. Lonely, sad, middle-aged women."

Nick's heart sank. "He doesn't marry them and murder them in the bath, does he?" he asked, half seriously.

"This is now, Nick, not a hundred years ago. He chats them up, gives them a good time in bed, makes them fall for him. Then he starts looking wistful and saying that if only he had a bit of capital he could set up his own West End studio and be the next David Bailey, or whoever it is now."

"And they say, 'Darling, you must let me finance you?'" He should have known: Ryder Drew with his con man's frank and fearless gaze.

"Then they write out a check for twenty, thirty, fifty grand, and bye-bye Andrew Ryder."

"They don't go to the police, surely?" Nick said.

"Two of them did, then backed out on further reflection. It makes them look so stupid, doesn't it? Pathetic, unloved, middle-aged women, believing that someone like him could really fall for them. They prefer to write off the loss to experience."

Nick thought about Lucy: so full of vigor and youthful ideals; looking ten years younger than her actual thirty-nine. *Pathetic, unloved, lonely, sad, middle-aged:* the words didn't fit. And yet she had been so low on his first visit to the cottage, hardly like the old Lucy at all. And so much happier on his next visit—a happiness which he was about to destroy.

"Did you get a description?" he asked. The inverted name was too much of a coincidence and so typical of the cocky criminal as to be almost pathological—as if the man in need of an alias had to retain a small part of his real self, his identity, in it. But he had to be sure before he went blundering into Lucy's future.

Bill read aloud from the piece of paper in his hand. "Short, skinny, blond hair, blue eyes, lots of charm."

"Short?" Nick queried. "Drew's a good six foot. And I wouldn't describe him as skinny, exactly, more sort of average." Coincidences did happen, after all.

Bill shrugged. "That's according to DI Crawford of Kensington CID."

Nick gave a short but mirthless laugh, his renewed hopes dashed. "Have you ever met Rob Crawford?"

"No. Why?"

"He's a great bruiser of a bloke, six foot eight in his stockinged feet, built like a brick shithouse. Almost everyone is a little runt in his book."

Bill looked annoyed. "Well, he ought to make a bit more of an effort with his descriptions then; he could mislead people."

"Never mind. Blond, blue eyes, charm. That's Ryder Drew, all right."

"So, who is he?" Bill asked.

"A friend of a friend of mine. And he's up to his old tricks, by the look of it, just changing his patch."

"What are you going to do about it?"

"Sleep on it."

He picked up a paper from his in-tray to indicate that the interview was at an end. Bill said he would call it a day and left. Nick put the paper back in his in-tray unread.

What did a real friend do in these circumstances? That

was easy: he told his friend the truth, lived with the pain he was causing, did what he could to help anesthetize it. But he would sleep on it, talk it over with Alison.

Which world did Lucy belong to now? Their world, or the other one—the submerged tenth?

When Nick got home that night, there was a note from Alison saying that she had gone to Exeter with Davey Jones to see a touring production of *Love's Labour's Lost*. He fished a moussaka out of the freezer and microwaved it while he made himself some salad. He ate his frugal meal with a glass of *Côtes du Rhône* and a good deal of thought. *Love's Labour's Lost*, eh?

> *The cuckoo then on every tree*
> *Mocks married men, for thus sings he:*
> *Cuckoo;*

It was still early, would not be dark for a couple of hours. If Alison wasn't around to give him her clear-sighted advice, then he'd find someone who was. There was Shirley, of course, with her cool analysis of every situation. He could go round and see if she was in.

Intending to do so, he got into his car and drove straight up to Colt's Head instead.

The paddock was almost empty when he arrived. Edwina stood in the middle of the field while Brimstone circled round and round her on a long rein. Felicity was riding Brimstone bareback, balancing with ease. She had her arms stretched out to either side as though being crucified. It looked rather boring, but one thing Edwina did not seem to lack was patience.

Felicity caught sight of him and waved. Edwina turned to see whom she was waving at and gave him a nod. Nick began to feel slightly giddy watching the interminable circle. "She's improving her seat." He hadn't heard Laura coming up behind him. "And her balance, for the gymkhana on Saturday." She offered him her cheek, and he pressed his lips to it hastily; he had not realized they were on kissing terms. She smelled of baby powder. "You coming?"

"I'll look in." He had already agreed to go with Alison.

"We'll have you in the saddle yet."

She stood next to him, watching her two eldest girls. Patience was in her arms, asleep. It was a happy, a restful, sight. Come to think of it, she was a much better person to turn to with Lucy's problems than either Shirley or Alison, both childless.

"I shall be sorry to lose Edwina," she said. "She may not have much to say for herself, but she's a hard worker."

"Why, where's she going?"

"To a racing stables at Lambourn. She's got a job there as a lad and, eventually, if all goes well, as a trainee jockey."

"Aren't you afraid for her?" he asked. "It seems like a rough business. I've read my Dick Francis."

"Broken legs are all in a day's work," she agreed, smiling, "but she must do something, and that's what she wants to do more than anything in the world. You can't mollycoddle people, not even your own children. It's better that she goes. But yes, I am afraid for her. Always."

At that moment almost a dozen horses and ponies came clattering in at the five-bar-gate, their riders—who included Grace and, on a Shetland pony, Amy—chattering and laughing. Patience woke up at the noise and yelled, "Wanna get down!"

"You've picked a bad time to come," Laura said ruefully. "The evening hack is back. There will be no peace now for at least an hour."

One of the girls was soaking wet, her long hair hanging damp about her sagging shoulders. Grace called out gleefully, "Mummy, mummy! Ptolemy rolled in the stream again."

"I don't believe it," Laura murmured.

Patience struggled out of her arms and began to dart fearlessly in and out of the forest of horses' legs. Her mother clapped her hands together and called, "Come on, ladies, let's have a bit of decorum. Mandy, come and get out of those wet things. You should know better than to let Tolly roll. Julie Binns, your seat is *awful*. Keep your back straight and your heels *directly* under your knees. Marsha Collins, your pony'll end up with a mouth like cast iron if you drag his bit about like that. Now, I want every one of these ponies groomed and fed and all of you ready for the off in half an hour. Got it! Half an hour!" She turned back to Nick. "Wishful thinking, I'm afraid, but it keeps them on their toes."

Felicity and Edwina gave up their exercise and went to help. Soon tired ponies were being sponged down and saddles were being wiped clean and hay was being proffered. Nick found himself holding the head of a skittish black horse at the behest of an assertive girl of about twelve who told him he might as well make himself useful if he was going to stand around watching. The horse kept butting him in the stomach in a manner he hoped was playful.

Laura's wishful thinking was not fulfilled, but the hack was cleared away within three-quarters of an hour, and when all the fond fathers had been and gone to whisk their weary daughters home to bed, Nick followed her into the house. It was now dusk. Patience had long since been put to bed, and Amy and Grace now followed without demur. Felicity and Edwina were out in the yard together, locking up for the night.

It was the evenings that were the best part of these hot days, he thought, when the temperature dropped at last and you cooled off and could loll around with friends and drink coffee or wine as if you were on holiday. In the twilight the moors exuded the safe, homely smell of heather.

"Drink?" Laura asked, proffering a bottle.

"No thanks. I've already had a couple of glasses and I'm driving."

"I have some orange juice."

"That would be lovely."

She poured some for him and wine for herself and they sat at the table together in companionable silence.

"You can't have been all that young when Patience was born," he said after a while.

She looked surprised. "Forty-three. I suppose it is old, but it's not as if she was my first."

"Does it get harder or easier?"

"Easier," she said, after much reflection. "When I just had Edwina, that was difficult. She wasn't an easy baby. But now she and Felicity are almost grown-up and look after the little ones. Why this sudden interest?"

"It's just that I have a friend—" He told her a little about Lucy, about the lively, active woman she had been, about her struggles with late motherhood.

"Is she a very special friend?" Laura asked with a coyness which did not fit her.

He smiled. "Not in the way you mean. At least, not now."

He was going to tell her about Alison's primary place in

his life, as he might have done at any point in their two weeks' acquaintance, but somehow that seemed a sidetrack from his real purpose in coming. He explained instead about Ryder Drew, or Andrew Ryder, and his dilemma, but, even as he spoke, his dilemma resolved itself, and he knew, as he had known all evening, that there was only one thing he could do.

"Leave well enough alone," Laura advised him when he had reached the end of his story. She laid her hand over his on the table top. "Let your friend be happy as long as it lasts. What you don't know can't hurt you."

But it can, he thought, it can. No, that wasn't the advice he had come to hear. He disengaged his hand, finished his orange juice, made his excuses, and left.

He got home at eleven and went straight to bed and fell asleep in no time. He woke up at once when Alison climbed into bed beside him.

"Wassa time?" he asked sleepily.

"Half past one."

"Christ! Must be the longest production of *Love's Labour's Lost* in the history of the world."

"Davey insisted on buying me dinner afterwards." She yawned noisily.

"He has that effect on me too," Nick said.

"Miaow, miaow, miaow." Alison began giggling inanely.

"You're drunk," Nick said.

"Of course I am. You don't think I'd lie here giggling like this if I was sober, do you?" She curled up against him and he winced.

"God! You're so cold!"

"You're very warm. Like a gigantic hot-water bottle." She pressed the full length of her body against his, and he turned over on his back and put his arms round her.

"Why're you so cold?" he asked.

"Davey has a vintage, open-top sports car."

"He would."

"He drove back from Exeter with the top down at about a hundred miles an hour."

"Bloody poseur."

She giggled again. "He flatters me."

"That's because he can't think of anything more intelligent to say. He looks like an old-English sheepdog and he has the conversational powers of an old-English sheepdog."

"He pays me compliments all the time. I like it."

"I pay you compliments!" Nick objected. "You have the most beautiful breasts in the world," he demonstrated. He had a quick feel to remind himself of their contours. They were just as cold as the rest of her, and the nipples stood out huge and hard. He abandoned his previous intention of going straight back to sleep and took one of them in his mouth to warm it.

> *Cuckoo, cuckoo—o word of fear,*
> *Unpleasing to a married ear!*

It didn't do much for a cohabiting one, come to that.

Lucy opened the door of High Wind Cottage to him the next morning, smiling, warm. He felt like a murderer.

"Come in," she said, "I've just made a saucepanful of Caribbean Surprise and it should have cooled off enough to drink by now."

"What is it?" Nick asked nervously.

"Just a sort of homemade lemonade—my mother's recipe."

"What's the surprise?"

"It wouldn't be a surprise if I told you."

He followed her into the kitchen, where she ladled two cupfuls of a strongly yellow liquid into tall glasses crammed with ice, and thence into the garden, where Hortense was lying on her back in a playpen, kicking her legs in the air and shouting something whenever a bird flew overhead.

"Drew not here today?" Nick asked, settling himself gingerly in a deckchair.

"He's gone."

"Gone?" he echoed stupidly.

"Back to London. Or off to find some other rich single woman he can ask for money."

"I see my errand here today is unnecessary, so I shall just

enjoy the sun and the company." Nick took a cautious sip of the lemonade. "It just tastes like lemonade," he remarked. "Very good homemade lemonade."

"That's because that's what it is."

"What's the surprise then?"

"That there isn't any rum in it. I'm not the first, then? I didn't suppose I could be."

"Not the first, the second, the third."

"Thank you for coming." She reached across and took his hand and held it for a moment. "It must have cost you a lot of heart-searching. It would have been so much easier just to mind your own business."

"Not really. You had to know the truth. There's no other way to live your life. 'You shall know the truth and the truth shall make you free,'" he quoted.

"I'm sorry you thought I was so gullible though, so stupid."

"Not gullible, certainly not stupid; a little . . . vulnerable lately."

"Hormones, that's all. That and the disruption, the complete change in lifestyle."

"But very real while it lasts."

"Better now."

"I wish there was something I could do about it, but he hasn't committed any crime. It's not illegal to ask your girlfriend for money."

"I don't really want anything done. I sent him on his way with no hard feelings on either side. It hasn't been wasted. Just having him around for a couple of weeks helped to lead me out of that dark wood I'd got myself lost in."

Nick stretched his legs out in front of him on the

parched grass, lighthearted in this unexpected freedom from unpleasant duty.

"This is bliss," he said.

"Make the most of it. I've put the cottage up for sale."

"What! Why?"

"This isn't me." She waved her hand at the picture-book surroundings. "Thatched roof, roses round the door, stone floors, inglenook fireplaces, beams, miles from anywhere. It sounds heavenly—straight off a chocolate box—but it isn't me. I can't imagine how I ever thought it was. Lucy Fielding is a town mouse, not a country mouse."

"Where will you go?"

"Back to Hopbridge. Not to the flat—Hortense must have a garden—but to a comfortable little semi within walk of the shops and the park, with replacement aluminium windows and patio doors." She laughed at Nick's face. "Not that bad, perhaps. One of those little Edwardian terraces down by the school will do us nicely."

"You're going back to work?"

"Not just yet although I might inquire about a bit of home tutoring. I'll go back properly in a year or two when Hortense is old enough for play school; part-time at first. It was important to me, you know, the teaching—planting a love of the French language and its literature in my pupils, watching it grow."

"I know."

"I wasn't meant to be a rich lady of leisure. I might just as well have given Ryder his fifty grand. I can afford it and if he wants it that badly—"

"Motherhood isn't exactly leisure," Nick pointed out.

"Was that his real name, by the way?"

"More or less."

"Only you feel so stupid moaning out a man's name in the heat of passion only to find out later that he was really called Herbert all along."

"I swear he wasn't really called Herbert."

"I shall take up my political activities again." Nick groaned. "Nothing extreme. Just the local Labour Party. Even the Thatcher woman cannot last forever—although she may think she can."

"I think she's probably immortal," he said.

"It was my social life," she went on, "those are my friends, my people. I don't know what made me think I could just break with the past, become a different person at the age of nearly forty. I must have been mad."

"Only temporarily deranged," he said.

"So drink another glass of Caribbean Surprise and then I shall have to shove you out. Hortense and I are going to an anti–poll tax rally in Taunton this lunchtime so we shall have to get off soon."

Nick began to laugh. "Dear Lucy, don't ever change . . . again."

"Here, you're not funny, are you?" Wayne asked, looking nervously round Nick's office. He glanced behind him at the closed door with its opaque glass panel.

"Funny?"

"The way you tried to cuddle me the other night, after the fire."

"I was just very pleased to see you in one piece."

"Only Cricky warned me. You know. To watch out for blokes who wanted to cuddle me."

"*Crick* did?"

"Yeah." Well, at least the man didn't believe in shitting on his own doorstep. "I didn't think you were," the boy said, satisfied with his reply. "Funny."

"Would you like me to get a WPC?" Nick asked, amused. "I did suggest your mum came—"

"No point in dragging her in," the boy said at once. "Anyway she wants to go to the hospital again to see Cricky. Silly mare."

"He's off the danger list, I hear."

"That's right. I suppose he gives her an interest in life."

"Can you remember who came to the house that day, Wayne? The day of the fire."

"Well, you did. And your funny friend with the camera. Where's he?"

"Gone home for the weekend."

"It's only Friday." The boy looked disapproving.

"He had to call in at his office in Exeter."

"Only he promised to show me his camera, let me have a go. It's a good one."

"I'll remind him on Monday. Apart from us, who came to the house?" Wayne made a face, indicating that the question did not interest him. "Milkman? Postman?"

"The milkman doesn't come any more 'cause he never got paid. I don't think there was any post—no, hang on, Cricky's social security check came. That was all."

"Wasn't it your birthday? Didn't you get any cards?"

"That was last week. It was just the kite got held up. Mum couldn't get it from a shop 'cause she had to pay for it over twenty weeks. Look, I can't really remember—the days are all the same in the holidays—but nobody unusual came all week, except for you, else I would've remembered. See? Sorry I can't be more help."

"All right, Wayne."

"Oh, and Pete came, of course."

"Pete?"

"Mr. Walters."

"Did he? Why?"

"He lives just down in Hopmouth. He often comes by to see I'm all right." The boy became confidential. "Dunno what he thinks is going to happen to me. They worry a lot, you know, grown-ups."

"It goes with the job."

"Sometimes he gives me a lift to school. Or back."

"And he came that day?"

"Yeah. 'Cause I hadn't gone into the school that day so he was worried. Honestly, he's such a fuss pot. I mean, it is the holidays. Cricky and Mum had gone out for a quick one at lunchtime, seeing as his check had arrived. They didn't get back till just before you came. I made him, Pete, a cup of tea, and he said something about me being too young to be left at home on my own. Honestly!" The boy's voice was indignant. "He didn't stay long, though. He cuddled me once, too."

Wayne frowned and Nick remembered how he, too, at the age of twelve had cringed when kissed and embraced by scented aunts and cousins, wriggled out of their clutches as soon as he could, and wiped their lipstick from his cheeks in disgust. Cuddles had been for sissies.

"I've never been in a real police station before," Wayne was saying. "Can I see the cells? Have you got any desperate criminals in them?"

Nick sat regarding him for a minute. The boy was unruffled by the events of Wednesday night. He had lost all his clothes except the ones he had been wearing on the cliff

201

that night, all his toys and games except his precious kite. He and his mother were sleeping in one room in a bed-and-breakfast hotel in town until more suitable accommodations could be found. But he didn't seem to mind; his little face was still cheeky and eager. His ginger hair had been roughly and ineptly cut, presumably by Martha, and stood up like a brush.

"Can I?" he repeated.

"I don't see why you shouldn't have a quick tour of the building," Nick said. "Although I'm afraid we don't get much in the way of desperadoes in Hopbridge. Come on."

Then she took you to the doctor when you were ten, as you had threadworms. Embarrassing for you, he said with a little laugh, but not dangerous. They liked places that were moist and warm. They would soon clear up with treatment.

Did he pause as he examined you, frown a little to himself? She was well-spoken and plausible, made some little joke about young girls and their ponies, and he laughed with relief. Riding, of course, the age-old excuse.

It felt like an adult conspiracy.

3

"You should stop flirting with Davey Jones," Nick said on Saturday morning. "He takes it seriously."

Alison tried on a look of wounded innocence, but it didn't suit her and she soon gave it up. "Oh . . . nonsense! It's just a game."

"Not to him. I wondered why he was looking so guilty whenever I spoke to him. I just about had him marked down as a child-porn customer. Then it dawned on me: he's embarrassed by my company because he fancies you and thinks you fancy him. The poor man is infatuated."

"Well, you're never around in the evenings at the moment; I've got to have someone to go around with. You needn't worry. All he ever does is talk about those bloody kids of his all the time. I know more about them than their mother does. Let me see: there's David junior who's twelve and at school in Hampstead and wants to be an England cricketer; then there's—"

"He's very vulnerable," Nick reminded her. "It's not long since his wife went off with another man."

"Who'd want to go to bed with a gynecologist anyway? He'd probably want to examine you before he screwed you."

"Alison! Really."

"He'd be down there, and you'd be wondering if he was comparing it with all the others he'd seen that day. You'd think it would put them off it for good, wouldn't you?"

"That's enough!"

The Hopbridge summer fête and gymkhana was in full swing when they reached Riverside Park at three o'clock that afternoon. The weather remained hot and sunny and there was a record turnout. Most of the people there were known to Nick and Alison, and their progress across the fields was slow as they stopped to greet old friends.

There was a predominance of little girls on ponies of every hue, all uncomfortably hot in riding jackets which they considered it bad form to remove. Some were even wearing gloves. The ponies had had their manes and tails laboriously plaited and sewn, and stepped out in immaculate tack being religiously warmed up for the big event—the under-thirteen jumping competition—which was the highlight of the show and the last event of the day.

A Chase-Me-Charlie game was taking place as they reached the arena. All the competitors followed each other over a single jump. Any pony that failed to clear the jump was eliminated, and then the height was raised for the next round. The game was reaching a climax with just three ponies left, one of which was ridden by Bill Deacon's youngest daughter Trudi—all apple-red cheeks and puppy fat.

"Come on, Trudi!" Nick yelled, caught up in the atmosphere of the place. Whether it was superior talent or Nick's encouragement, Trudi won the game. She was awarded a red rosette, and her sturdy pony was rewarded with a sugar lump. They could see Bill and Susie with Sarah and Chrissie at the other side of the ring cheering and waving.

More games followed as a procession of small girls with the very occasional small boy among them wove their ponies in and out of lines of poles or bobbed for apples or played musical sacks. There were, inevitably, tears, and a row threatened to erupt over the Prettiest Pony class, where the judge selected a flighty and overbred mare with obvious dashes of Arab blood over any more homely specimen. Local feeling was affronted by this snub to the Exmoors with their short strong backs, their straight shoulders, and their family trees stretching back to the Domesday Book; although a disinterested observer would have had to agree that, with their mealy noses and toad eyes and the distinct yellowish tinge to their pelt, they were not about to win any beauty contests.

"God, this takes me back," Alison said.

"I wonder where Laura is," Nick said, "and Felicity. You'd think she'd be taking part in some of these games at least."

"I daresay she thinks herself too grand for kid's stuff like this. Yes, look. There she is, doing the practice jump. With Laura giving her some last-minute coaching."

Nick looked in the direction she was pointing and waved, but they were absorbed in what they were doing and neither of them saw him. Around them all was bustle and movement as the gymkhana events were cleared away, fresh straw was strewn all over the arena, and the show jumping fences were hastily erected.

"Will you look at that!" Alison said, pointing in the opposite direction.

Nick followed the line of her finger again. He saw Lucy in the distance with—surely it couldn't be—with Davey Jones. But there could be no mistaking that broad figure, that fat blond mustache. Hortense was hoisted on Davey's shoulder and had, for once, abandoned her laid-back demeanor and was shouting with excitement as they stood watching pink and white candyfloss being expertly wound round a stick.

"He's found a substitute for those kids he's missing so badly," Nick commented. "Blow me. What an ill-assorted couple."

"Where do you suppose they met?"

"Anti–poll tax rally?" he suggested.

"What? Davey Jones?"

"Perhaps he's not as boring and predictable as I thought."

It was now past five o'clock and the ponies' shadows were growing longer on the dry grass. The main event—the jumping competition—was reaching its final jump off against the clock with four girls left to compete, two of whom were Felicity and Trudi. Trudi, on her stocky, middle-aged Larkspur, was the first to jump.

She was going well for the first half of the course, making good time over a series of simple obstacles which she cleared with ease. Larkspur slowed and wheeled in the farthest corner, stamped his hooves twice on the ground with enthusiasm, and, urged on by Trudi's booted feet, pricked up his ears and made for the three-bar-spread at a gallop.

"That's a spooky fence," Alison said.

"A what?"

"There's something about it the horses don't like. I noticed it earlier. They all hesitate there. I think it may just be that they come round that corner and find the sun right in their eyes. Steady! Oooh!"

An echoing Oooh! of dismay went up from the crowd as Larkspur refused at the last second, his front feet digging firmly into the well-churned earth in front of the spread, his head bent nearly to the ground. Trudi almost went straight over his head but clung bravely on and somehow managed to avoid an ignominious, and probably painful, plunge onto the fence. Undaunted, she pulled him round, cantered back to give herself a sufficient run at it, and tried again.

The Oooh! on this occasion was even louder as Larkspur veered away this time, bypassing the hated spread by galloping round it. Trudi's face was now a picture of shame and misery.

"She'll be into penalty time points in a minute," Alison remarked, "as well as six faults for refusals. She's not giving up though."

Trudi took Larkspur back to the same corner, did a half pirouette to turn him as quickly as possible, and urged him at the fence at an even faster pace, leaning forward into his mane, whispering threats or entreaties in his ear. A judicious kick at the right moment took the little pony sailing over the fence to thunderous applause from the crowd. They took the rest of the course at something approaching a gallop and without further incident to finish just within the alloted time for six faults.

"Should we go and commiserate?" Nick asked. "Or is it a case of least said, soonest mended?" But Alison was already walking across to the Deacon family group. Nick hurried after her.

"Rotten luck, Trudi," he called, as he drew level with them. He pushed his way through a circle of friends and well-wishers.

She took her hat off and gave him a weak smile, sadly disappointed but trying very hard to be a good sport. "It's just one of those things. Horses have good memories. Once something bad happens to them somewhere they never forget it so, once they refuse at a fence, they're inclined to just go on and on refusing."

"Never mind, love." Bill hugged his roly-poly youngest daughter. "It's the taking part that counts."

"Of course it is," Alison lied heartily.

"Let's cool old Larkspur off, and then I'll buy you an ice cream," Bill went on.

"Thanks, Dad." The biggest ice cream in the world would not compensate her for her letdown, but she knew it was her father's way of showing he cared.

"The others may do worse," Sarah pointed out, taking Larkspur's bridle from her sister and offering him a sugar cube. "Here you are, old boy, rot your teeth. You did your best."

"That's right," Alison said. "The opera isn't over until the fat lady sings."

"It's that stuck-up Marsha Collins to jump now," Chrissie said, breaking into the conversation, which was unusual for her. She was very fond of her baby sister and hated to see her disappointed. "Let's all hope she falls off. Do her good."

"Chrissie!" her mother rebuked her. "That hardly qualifies as good sportsmanship."

Nick, following Chrissie's pointing finger, saw the bossy girl with the black horse trotting into the arena, the girl who had told him to make himself useful after the hack, Derek Collins's eldest daughter. She was dressed as if posing for a riding magazine in white jodhpurs and a black coat and, unlike the other girls, carried a small springy whip in her right hand. He could not help silently repeating Chrissie's wish that she might fall off.

She did not oblige either of them, but she did bring down a bar at the very first fence, a simple upright brush designed to ease the competitors in.

"Hurrah!" Chrissie mimed behind her mother's back.

Marsha gave her pony a sharp crack across the neck with her whip which brought murmurs of disapproval from the crowd so that when another fence clattered to the ground in the treble at the end of the course there was little sympathy to be had. The loudspeaker announced, to hoots of derision from Chrissie and a quiet smile from Nick, that Miss Marsha Collins, with eight faults, lay in second place.

The other girl brought down only one fence but had a refusal at the same three-bar-spread that had been Trudi's bugbear to take second place with seven faults, pushing the frowning Marsha down into third. Trudi, with ice cream melting over her hands and mouth, was beginning to look more optimistic.

There was only Felicity to jump now.

Nick was not sure whom he was rooting for—old friends in the shape of the Deacons or new ones in the shape of the beleaguered Bottones. There was a saying, wasn't there? Something about new friends being silver but old ones being gold. He decided he'd better just keep quiet.

Everyone in Hopbridge seemed to be crowded round the arena now as Felicity, looking very young, rode proudly into the ring on Brimstone. Nick looked around for Laura.

Instead of joining the crush at the ringside, she had climbed up on a bale of straw a few yards back, from where she had a clear view of the action. She was gnawing at a thumbnail, while looking outwardly calm.

Tension mounted as Brimstone caught a parallel bar with his back legs, rocking it so that it looked as if it must certainly fall away. It trembled for some time before settling back in its rest. A moan of disbelief went up and Felicity lost a little time by glancing back to see what had happened. She wiped her brow theatrically in mock relief and galloped on to the laughter and support of the crowd. Brimstone did not spook at the three-bar-spread and hesitated only briefly at the makeshift water jump, as if he didn't fancy getting his feet wet. He cleared the last treble—an upright and two oxers—with ease and cantered home to the cheers of the onlookers.

"A clear round for Miss Felicity Bottone," the loudspeaker proclaimed as thunderous applause broke out round the ring.

"Brimstone is such a brave little jumper," Alison said. "He hurls himself at those fences as if he were running the Grand National, as if he didn't know the meaning of the word fear. I can't imagine what can have given him the heebie-jeebies in the stable the other day."

Derek Collins's hissing whisper could be heard urgently promising his angry daughter a new and better pony for next year.

"A bad workwoman blames her tools," Alison muttered into Nick's ear.

Felicity sat pink with pride as the judge pinned the winner's rosette to Brimstone's bridle and handed her a tiny silver cup. She shook hands with Trudi, who was collecting her blue rosette with a sporting smile. Then she rode from the arena, holding her cup aloft, to further cheers and clapping. Laura stepped forward to hold the pony's head as her daughter flung herself off and did a victory dance around both of them.

"Another cup to clean," she remarked drily.

Then Felicity spotted Nick. "Uncle Nick!" She ran across and threw her arms round his neck. "Did you see? My first red rosette."

Laura followed more slowly, leading the pony. She stared as she realized that Alison and Nick were together and that they were holding hands. "I didn't know you two knew each other."

They smiled into each other's eyes.

"Slightly," he said.

"Very slightly," she said.

"Well, well." Laura turned away from them. "You learn something new every day. Come on, Feckless. What's a good horsewoman's first consideration, even if she has just won a red rosette?"

Felicity knew the answer to that one. "Her horse."

"Right. So let's get Brimstone unsaddled and give him a nice drink of water and a short feed and see if his legs need padding."

She nodded coolly to Nick and Alison and led horse and daughter away.

"You never said you knew Alison Hope."

The soft voice whispered in Nick's ear just as he reached the front of the long queue in the tea tent half an hour later.

"Yes, dear?" the tea lady asked sharply, making it clear that she would not tolerate any dawdling.

"Can I get you anything, Laura?"

"Just tea."

"Three teas, please, and a slice of that ginger cake."

He delved in his trouser pocket for change and somehow managed to pick three plastic cups and a paper plate up in his hands. They retreated to a quiet corner of the marquee where there was a handy table with a soiled paper cloth and many generations of crumbs.

"Ooh," he said, putting the cups down and blowing on his scalded hands.

"You never said you knew Alison," she repeated, taking a cup and wrapping her small hands round it, distending it out of shape.

"In the biblical sense? Every nook and cranny." She couldn't help smiling at that. "Seriously—we've been living together for nearly three years."

"You told me you were a bachelor."

"So I am. I didn't mean to deceive you, Laura. If you had designs on my body, you should have said."

She laughed and shook her head. "I never would have guessed it, though. You're such an unlikely couple. So different. Alison is like quicksilver: so impulsive, so feminine."

"Do you think so?" he said, startled. "That's not the general view. Most people in the valley would tell you that she's about as soft and feminine as an iron railing."

"You of all people know better than that."

"Yes." He smiled. "I do. I'm sorry you think us an unlikely couple. I think we're two halves of the same person. When she's away from me I feel . . . incomplete."

"That's nice." She looked at him thoughtfully. "There aren't many men willing to declare their feelings like that."

"I don't see why not. Why should any man be ashamed of loving a woman?"

"It's not considered masculine to be uxorious. You notice there's no female equivalent of uxorious, don't you? I
can never quite work out what that means. It may be it's
taken for granted that women worship their husbands or it
may be it's taken for granted that they don't. What do you
think, Nick?"

He smiled uneasily, unable to interpret her strange
mood. "She's a good woman," Laura went on. He didn't
know how to answer her still. Alison was strong and bright
and honest and generous but *goodness* seemed too abstract
a concept for the tail end of the twentieth century.

"Look," he said, "I must take her her tea before it gets
cold and her cake, since she's allegedly starving." He laid a
hand on her arm. "I'll see you soon, Laura."

"Yes. Very soon."

She stood watching him as he left the tent, watching with
the expression of someone scratching an open wound.

4

Nick lowered the *Sunday Times* Review section the next morning. "What was that you were saying yesterday," he asked, "at the gymkhana, about Brimstone having the heebie-jeebies?" They were sitting on the terrace in their dressing gowns, surrounded by pieces of Sunday newspaper and the remains of a late breakfast. The sky was cloudless and the day promised to be idyllic, but they were a little blasé about it after all these weeks. Alison took another sip of her tea and considered for a long time before she replied.

"I've been thinking about that."

She had been thinking of what Trudi had said about the way horses remembered places where they had suffered or been afraid, of Brimstone being struck with terror at the stable door, of spaghetti Westerns. But she had been too warm and sleepy and comfortable to turn this kaleidoscope of ideas in search of a recognizable shape, to voice these thoughts.

Besides, they were preposterous.

"Nick."

Laura appeared through the door from the passage at

the far end of the kitchen. "When I said yesterday I'd see you again soon, I didn't think it would be quite as soon as this. You are welcome, as ever."

They were alone in the room. Outside, the stable yard was busy with Sunday morning traffic: setting out on hacks, practicing jumping or basic dressage in the paddock. The kitchen was a silent haven from all this activity.

"Hello, Laura." He did not advance into the room but stood in the doorway: still, unsmiling.

She came forward and, before he could anticipate her move or stop her, hugged him tightly. He shrank from her, like the time he had turned an exuberant handspring in the garden on receiving his "O" level results and made fleshly contact with a huge, black, horned slug. She stepped back and looked at him with challenge in her eyes.

"I wondered how long it would be before you put it all together. When I found out you knew Alison, I realized it was only a matter of time." She smiled faintly and shook her head as though admonishing her youngest child. "I tried to warn you, Nick, so many times. I told you to leave well alone, not to meddle, but you wouldn't listen."

"What I didn't know wouldn't hurt me?"

"That's right."

"'Arturo is dead; let me bury him and get on with my life?'"

"Why not? You can't bring him back. Your meddling might have wrecked a whole lot more lives, children's lives. I thought that was what you wanted to avoid. I thought they were the ones who had to be protected at all costs. Isn't that what all this has been about?"

"Not at *any* cost."

"That must be where we differ, you and I. You have no children of your own."

"So people keep pointing out," he said, angry now, "but I'm still entitled to my opinion."

"Wait. Wait until you have held your own flesh and blood in your arms, so small and helpless and trusting. Wait until you have heard her cry for milk and comfort; then, later, come home unexpectedly to hear her crying out in confusion and terror and pain, to learn that it is not the first time, that it has been going on for *three years.*"

"You didn't know, suspect, guess, before that?"

"No. It all started shortly after Felicity was born, you see. I was absorbed with the new baby. When you're breast-feeding, nothing seems real except that demanding mouth, so tiny but with the suction force of an industrial pump. She became more withdrawn, certainly, but she had always been a quiet child. I put it down to sibling jealousy, to no longer being the center of my world after seven years."

"And when you did find out, you did nothing? You didn't go to the police? You didn't at least send him packing?"

She shook her head sadly. "I sent her away instead."

"I want to get it all straight, Laura" he said. "You used Brimstone to hang Arturo? I can hardly believe it."

"It's one of the oldest ways there is, ever since man first tamed the horse. Haven't you ever seen Clint Eastwood being bundled into the saddle, the noose put round his neck, the horse driven away with a slap on the rump? It's all so simple. Only in his case, he always walks away from it; not like in real life."

"It's . . . devilish."

"It was hard on Brimstone, certainly. Animals know, somehow, when there's a death, especially a violent one. They can sense the strong emotions in the humans on the scene. Dogs do it; horses, too. He was terrified at the time, it was all we could do to hold him. Then, when Edwina tried to take him into the stable a few days later, while Alison was here, he just went crazy." She stood leaning against the door jamb, a faint smile on her lips, remembering. "I knew Alison would be bound to say something about it, perhaps not yesterday or today but one day and soon. And that you, of all people, would see at last."

"Thank you for the compliment although I don't really deserve it."

"She's below the age of criminal responsibility, you know."

"I know. But you aren't and neither is Edwina."

"Edwina." She sighed. "It was all for Edwina. Felicity would do anything to protect her. It was as if she was the big sister and Edwina the child."

"That was what fooled me, I think. The knowledge that Edwina wasn't technically a child; that, at sixteen, she was over the age of consent."

"She was a child at the time, of course. That's partly why she is the way she is: backward, intellectually and emotionally retarded, frightened of her own shadow. I sent her away to boarding school, to get her away from Arturo, made sure she spent the holidays with friends. Then, by the time she left school this summer, came back here, he wasn't living with us and I thought she'd be safe. Then he came back."

How stupid he had been. It was always so much more likely to be the stepfather than the father. It wasn't Felicity who had needed examining by Dr. Slater.

"And Felicity knew?"

"Edwina confided in her. She told her everything—quite recently, I think. When Arturo came home, she was afraid

217

he would start again. Or she may have been afraid he would turn to her or Grace or even the little ones. She decided to take action. She's an intelligent, determined, and logical child. She knew there was only one way to make sure Edwina would be safe for good."

"Tell me what happened that night. One step at a time. I need to see it in my head."

"Arturo came home from the magistrates' court as I told you originally, went straight to the stable, and started drinking. I couldn't sleep that night, worrying what I was going to do about him, about all of it—"

One o'clock in the morning, a noise out in the stable yard where nothing stirs at night. It sounds like muffled hoofbeats on the cobbles. Laura goes to the window, looks out. Felicity is leading Brimstone towards the stable, his hooves swaddled in rags of sacking. Edwina is trailing along behind as if she doesn't quite grasp what's going on. She holds a torch.

Laura dresses quickly and runs down. Arturo is dead drunk up in the hay loft, unconscious, slumped across the camp bed fully clothed where he fell. She realizes now what they have come to do, what Felicity has come to do, and that they will not be able to do it without her help. She joins them silently, saying nothing, climbs the steps into the loft, beckons Edwina to join her, which she does, obedient as ever.

Laura and Edwina lower Arturo from the hatch onto Brimstone's back, one on each arm. Felicity sits behind him to hold him upright. Poor little Brimstone is groaning under the weight, but he stands there as good and as patient as ever.

Laura throws the leading rein over the beam and loops it round his neck with a sliding knot. It is not easy. His head flops forward, then backward, leaving his face exposed, va-

cant, pointing up towards the hatch. Laura leans over and plants a last kiss on that flaccid mouth. His eyes open for a second but it is a reflex, that's all. There is no understanding.

Felicity jumps off, leads Brimstone away. She is as cool as can be throughout, has perhaps not really taken in the consequences of her actions as children may not. Edwina is acquiescent, as ever. Laura is the one who is in a sweating panic. For a moment she thinks she may faint and pitch forward out of the hatch and die on the sharp cobbles, and for a second she thinks that may be no bad thing. Then she pulls herself together, admonishes herself.

Brimstone slides away from under the drunken man's limp body. He is already afraid as the noose tightens and a kicking leg catches him on the flanks. His ears start back. It is all Felicity, now aided by Edwina, can do to hold him. He whinnies in panic. An answering, a reassuring, whinny comes from the stall round the corner where Goldie had been asleep but has been roused by the commotion. It seems to comfort him: he is not, after all, alone with these humans and their madness.

It takes longer than she had imagined, longer than any of them had imagined, except Edwina, who has no imagination and had not given the matter any thought. She sends the two girls away, and they take the little gray pony out and make a fuss of him while their mother waits almost a quarter of an hour to see it ended.

She places the Windsor chair, oh so carefully, just where he would have kicked it if that had been how it was done.

" . . . You know, if horses could vomit, I think little Brimstone would have vomited that night," she concluded. "I felt bad about that."

She felt bad about that, he thought. Stringing her husband up, she could cope with that, but she felt bad about frightening the horse.

"Was that really how it happened?" he asked.

"It's one version," she replied.

He understands: he can never know the full truth—that is the most bitter fact of every closing investigation, one he has become reconciled to over the years. No judge or jury can look into a killer's heart. This story does not reflect so badly on her; she was not the instigator; she was swept along in the vengeful passion of that hot night. It may be that she needs to remember it that way.

She continued. "Afterwards Felicity said, 'That's done then'. She knew Edwina was in no more danger—or Grace or Amy or Patience. We all came back in and went to bed until it was time for me to get up and find him and ring the police. It was a genuine shock, somehow, opening the stable door and hearing Goldie neigh out a greeting and seeing him hanging there; as if it might all have been illusion and he might be gone by now. She misses him, though, Felicity; she was his favorite, his pet."

She looked at him steadily. "We are alone. You have no witnesses to what I have just told you. You have no evidence. There is not even, officially, a case to investigate; you told me that."

"How do you know I haven't just taped everything you've said?"

"Why do you think I came and hugged you like that? You're not 'wired up'."

"You think of everything, don't you?"

"I try to. Besides," she smiled, "that is not your way."

He remembered how she had seemed from the first to know him, to understand him. She had used that knowledge. She knew that, whatever hand he played, it would not be underhand.

"Do you realize, at least, what you have done, the consequences of your actions?" he said.

"What was the alternative? I had failed to protect my daughter. I didn't stop my little girl from being assaulted by her stepfather. This was the only thing left I could do for her—for all of them." A note of passion came into her voice, of despair. "Is there something wrong with me? That I can't attract a decent, honest man—a man like you, perhaps." She held out her bare wrists, as narrow and as white as a girl's. "Where are the handcuffs? Aren't you supposed to caution me?"

"Oh no, Laura. I'm not playing that game. If I arrest you now, charge you, you'll be acquitted for lack of evidence, and then you'll be beyond the reach of justice. I know you too well to believe I can get an admissible confession out of you."

"Quite correct."

And even if he could, juries—he had found—had grown reluctant to convict on confession alone these last few years, and he had been one of the first to welcome this reluctance.

"This case will stay open," he told her, "if only in my head, for as long as it takes. You will never really be able to call yourself safe. One day, I shall light on a little piece of evidence, some tiny part of the jigsaw puzzle, which will betray you. I shall keep on looking. On that day, I shall come back for you with my handcuffs and my cautions. I shall be watching you. If you so much as park on a yellow line or take your library books back late, I shall know about it. Each night as you lie down to sleep easy in your bed, Laura, remember that."

"I had not imagined you could be so vindictive." He had unnerved her. "There are many who would say, after what he did, that hanging was too good for him."

"We have laws, lawyers, policemen to deal with men like Arturo."

"Oh yes! Policemen, social workers, all sorts of do-gooders. But they can rarely see inside the opaque walls of the family home, let alone reach in."

"Once any civilized society gives in to the lynch-mob mentality, it's finished."

She shook herself. "You frighten me."

"I'm glad."

She crossed to the coat stand and reached into the pocket of a black trench coat hanging there. "You'd better take this, as a sort of consolation prize. It's that list you wanted so badly—Arturo's shopping list." She held it out to him.

"Was it in that raincoat pocket all the time?" he asked.

"Oh, don't go shouting at your men. I hid it 'about my person' while they were searching the place. They could never have found it, short of strip-searching me. I thought the quicker the whole fuss died down the better. But it doesn't matter now. You can have it."

She corrected herself with gentle irony. "What I mean, of course, is that I just happened to find it yesterday evening, stuffed into one of the legs of the water trough in the paddock and hurried to give it to you like the good, law-abiding citizen I am. Oh, and the photographs come from North Africa, via Italy."

"You knew, didn't you? All along?"

"I thought it a safer . . . outlet for him."

"Other people's children?"

"Better than mine. I thought it would help to keep his hands off my daughters."

Nick glanced at the first three names on the list, then stuffed it in his pocket. He burst out, unable to stop himself.

"Oh, Laura!"

"Don't pity me, Nick. Anything but that."

As he drove out of the yard, wrenching his car into gear with angry movements, Felicity was sitting on the five-bar-gate and gave him a happy wave. He forced his grim mouth into a smile for her. English law did not accept that a nine-year-old child was capable of *mens rea*—that malice before the fact, that element of responsibility, that any criminal charge necessitated. He gave her the benefit of the doubt. There were children who killed and went on to become adults who killed; others, like Mary Bell, seemed to survive to live a normal life. It was out of his hands, but he wished he could see this sunny nine-year-old life, full of innocent potential, out from under the influence of her mother.

In his rear-view mirror he could see Laura, standing out-side the stable block, watching him leave. As with his first glimpse of her, he was struck by the strength, the authority, of her slight but erect figure.

It was the last time he was ever to see her.

5

"Now that you've finally accepted the suicide verdict on Bottone," Shirley said the next morning, since that was what he had told her, "perhaps I can have some of your attention on this arson case, since I don't seem to be getting anywhere."

Nick sat down wearily at his desk. "I suppose I asked for that," he said. "I—"

The door opened and Jim Humbleby shambled in. This was to be his last day in Hopbridge, and he had a few loose ends to tidy up. "Just looked in to say goodbye really," he said. "Suicide, arson, pornography. I can do a whole series of articles on just these two weeks. Keep me going for ages. It's incredible what your lot get up to in these little back-of-beyond places, isn't it? Still waters running deep, eh? I've had a very profitable stay."

"What will you write exactly, Jimbo?" Nick asked, trying to pay attention, to take his mind off things, glad only that Jim didn't know the half of it.

"Oh, you know the sort of thing. *Detective plays lord of the manor at snooty girlfriend's house. Fails to protect mentally ill woman from lynch-mob arsonist. Uses police resources to pursue private projects of his own.*"

"Now wait a minute—" He had Nick's full attention now.

"What?" Humbleby was smiling unpleasantly, his beige face pinkened. "What did you think would happen when your Assistant Chief Constable (Admin)—or whatever pompous title he goes by—approached my editor to set up a public relations exercise for the police? That we'd just be your posing mouthpieces?"

"I trusted you."

"You patronized me, you mean."

"You little shit," Shirley said, angry for Nick, not for herself.

"Oh, yes. 'Poor old Jim. Very good, Jim. We'll make a detective of you yet, Jim.' Dixon of Dock Green lives on in Hopbridge—was that was I was supposed to write?"

"The theory as I was told it was that you were going to write the truth," Nick pointed out. "No whitewash but no mud-chucking either."

"Good news is no news."

"I had begun to look upon you as a friend," Nick said.

"Remember I told you I was the New Reporter?"

"I remember."

"You've heard of the New Man?"

"Of course."

"Sensitive, caring, not afraid of his feelings, helps with the washing up? He finds he gets more nookie that way? Well, I get more stories this way." He got up. "Time I was going. Next stop, Fleet Street."

"I think you mean the Isle of Dogs," Nick said. "Appositely."

"I'll send you copies of the features. My editor's gonna love them. He can't stand your ACC."

"Just a minute." Nick got to his feet and came round the desk.

"What is it? I've got a deadline to meet."

"Where were you on the night of Wednesday, July the twelfth, Humbleby?"

"Eh?"

"Well?"

"Wednesday . . . At your place, with Milady Hope. Being patronized."

"Not then, later. Around one o'clock in the morning. Or a week after that, Wednesday, July the nineteenth? Same sort of time. Where were you then?"

"Have you gone raving mad?"

Nick continued to advance with Humbleby, by far the smaller man, retreating before him. Shirley moved to block the doorway, and the two men did a couple of circuits of the little office. Nick's expression was unreadable, and his silence began to menace the reporter more than words ever could.

"You can't keep me here," he squeaked. "Let me out. You're mad!"

"I don't think so. Let's just look at the facts, shall we? The arson was following me about. I remarked as much to Colin Burcombe, but I didn't mean it literally at the time."

"I should think not!"

"But let's just look at it literally for a moment. Who was it who was actually following me about all that time? You were: James Humbleby, the New Reporter. You were with me when I saw Mrs. Tyson. You remarked that she must have known what her husband was up to—"

"He said that to me, too," Shirley put in. "Like he thought she ought to be punished as well."

"When we left the school, you said you hoped the pedophiles got what was coming to them—"

"Now, hang on a minute—"

"You were with me when I searched Crick's place, when I interviewed him. That very night, the place went up in flames. Took half the terrace with it. It was a miracle someone wasn't killed. Bit of a coincidence, wouldn't you say?"

"But that's all it is, a coincidence. I was at the hotel, both nights, developing pictures until about midnight and then I went to bed. Ask the hotel."

"They don't have an all-night reception at the Old Railway Hotel. Guests get a key if they're going to be out after eleven. You must have got one on the night you came to dinner at Hope Cottage. Thanks for abusing my hospitality, by the way."

"It's not true. It wasn't me. I haven't got a car, can't even drive."

"Sez you!"

"I can't! How was I supposed to get up to Hopcliff in the middle of the night?" Nick was forced to admire the way the man kept his wits about him under stress.

"You don't think I'm going to be put off by a little detail like that, do you? Give me one good reason why I shouldn't arrest you on suspicion of arson, of attempted murder? How'd you like a firsthand view of the cells? That'd make a good story, wouldn't it? And a blow by blow"—he banged his fist into his other palm—"account of being on the receiving end of a CID interrogation. Your editor'll love that."

"Course," Shirley added, "if you get sent down for it you can do a series of articles about life in prison. Riveting stuff, I'd imagine."

"I . . . I . . . " Humbleby had arrived back at Nick's desk in his original starting position and sat down in a crumpled beige heap. "You can't be serious."

"'I like a good bonfire myself,'" Nick quoted. "I bet you do. My case is getting stronger and stronger all the time. Didn't it occur to you that you might kill someone—perhaps that little boy Wayne?"

"That's your proof that I didn't do it!" Humbleby said angrily. "That kid could have been me at that age. Like I'd risk his life!"

"I'm expected to believe all that guff about your unhappy childhood, am I? The alcoholic and violent father, the years in care. It's just another tale along with all the rest you've spun me over the past fortnight."

"That was the truth." Humbleby sought around for more proof. "And that's not my voice on that 999 tape. You know it isn't. It's local. It's rough. It doesn't sound anything like me. Even you can't make out that it does. And I was with you when Mrs. Tyson got the threatening phone call and you said that was the same voice, remember?"

"I said it might have been."

"No, you didn't. You said you'd bet a year's salary on it."

"All right! Get out!"

"What!"

"I said, Get out. Buzz off, Bumble Bee."

Shirley stood to one side, amused, as Humbleby leaped to his feet and wrenched open the door. He paused, said "Tough bitch, no wonder you haven't got a boyfriend" to her, and left. They could hear his feet almost running down the corridor.

Shirley began to laugh. "Revenge is sweet."

"It all goes to show you should never trust a man who

wears a cardigan," Nick said, "and so much for my built-in bullshit detector."

"Thank goodness I didn't agree to the 'in-depth' interview he wanted to do with me. I'd probably have ended up as Sexy Shirley, the Siren of the Force."

"No, he couldn't spell 'siren.'"

Nick took the photograph of himself that Humbleby had given him out of the drawer, tore it into little pieces, and put it in the waste paper bin. He took the sheets of paper Laura had given him out of his pocket again, smoothed them out and examined them.

"I'll be with you in a few minutes, Shirley. I've just got to go and have a word with Mr. Grey about this."

"Sir, I've got that list of names and addresses of Bottone's customers at last."

Reg was, as usual, looking worriedly out of the window. He turned into the room with a heavy sigh. "If we don't get some rain soon, it'll be the end for my roses," he said. So that was it! That was why Reg had been looking as if he had the cares of the world on his shoulders for the past few weeks; his roses were thirsty. "Sorry, Nick. What were you saying?" Nick repeated his remark and handed over the sheets of paper. Reg's eye slid quickly down the first one and he said without much emphasis, "Bloody Hell."

"Yes, sir."

"What are you going to do with them?"

"Nothing much I can do."

"Nothing?"

"They're a list of names on a piece of paper I got from Laura Bottone. It could be anything, in theory. A list of subscribers to a charity or something. Bottone is dead. I haven't a chance of a conviction against any of this lot. I wouldn't get a search warrant even."

"It's not the first time, Nick. There'll always be a handful who escape justice."

More than a handful in this case, Nick thought. He recalled Bottone's laughing wordplay in the interview room three weeks ago. Counting Laura, more like an armful.

"I shall pay them all a little visit over the next few weeks, though," he said. "Very informal, ask them why their names were on a list in the possession of a trafficker in child porn. They'll bluster, swagger, maybe threaten. But I'll know and they'll know I know; that may be enough."

"It will have to do."

"I think we might quietly take Mr. Collins off the duty-solicitor list, though."

"I can't believe it—the chap's a Rotarian. He's married, got three children—nice little girl, mad about ponies."

"Yes, sir." He wondered if Reg ever listened to a word that was said to him. He'd already told him that most pedophiles were married and had children of their own. And where did he think Collins had met Bottone?

He remembered the gymkhana: Derek Collins desperate to placate his unpleasant daughter, to make amends for her disappointment, promising her a new pony. No doubt he would promise her anything in return for her silence. The girl was spoiled, all right, but not in the way Nick had thought.

"All this mess," Reg was saying. "Arson, respectable family men committing professional suicide—and all for what? A few mucky pictures."

Nick had had enough. "Stay there," he shouted, to the

superintendent's amazement. "Don't move a muscle."

He ran down the stairs two at a time to his own office, ignored Shirley's "That was quick," unlocked the large drawer of his desk, removed a dozen glossy photographs, put them in a cardboard folder, started out of the room, came back and locked the drawer again with an apologetic glance at her, and ran back up the stairs.

"What the hell's got into you?" Reg demanded.

"Sit down, sir." Nick spread the topmost photograph down on the desk in front of the superintendent. "You'll need to." Reg was too surprised not to obey. "*Mucky picture* number one."

Reg found himself staring into the face of an angelic-looking fair-haired boy of about eight. A bruise was spreading across his left cheek; both eyes were closed fast but there was a pained smile stuck on his mouth; with him, a man with deliberately blurred features.

"My God!" he gasped.

"*Mucky picture* number two."

A small girl of Oriental appearance cowered on a rug wearing a bikini in lurex-type material, the top concealing nonexistent breasts. One arm was flung over her face in a vain attempt to protect her frail self from a snarling dog. Above it she gazed at the camera with blank eyes.

Reg looked away. "You've made your point, Inspector."

"I have the next one in this particular sequence, if you'd like to see it."

"No," Reg said weakly. "No, I wouldn't."

"Not exactly 'What the butler saw,' is it, sir?"

"I said you've made your point." Reg brushed the photos away, out of his line of vision. "My God!" he said again.

Nick put the photos back in the cardboard folder and

stuck his head out of the door into the outer office. "Mrs. Jewson, do you think the superintendent might have a glass of water? I think the heat's getting to him."

Reg Grey recovered his spirits quickly enough now the pictures were out of sight and Mrs. Jewson was clucking over him. Nick waited until his cheeks had returned to their normal florid color then murmured that he would be off, as he had work to do. Reg signaled him to stay and thanked Mrs. Jewson politely but firmly to send her away.

"When is the Bottone inquest reopening?" he asked.

"Thursday."

"I trust you won't be asking for another adjournment."

"It appears not."

"Good. Since we're all agreed that suicide is the only logical explanation." Reg relaxed and flexed back in his chair. "I gather your shadow has gone," he went on. "The ACC (Admin) is very keen to see the result of this experiment. He's hoping to repeat it in other units. No problems?"

"Well, actually, sir—"

"Good. Good."

Reg fell back to the contemplation of his dying roses, and Nick did not have the strength to pursue the matter further. There was nothing Reg could do about Humbleby anyway, nothing any of them could do.

A worthless list of names; a stab in the back from a supposed friend; a real friend guilty of murder, but inviolable; Ryder Drew free to move on to his next victim. Nick had never felt so impotent.

6

"You don't really believe that Jim was the arsonist, then?" Shirley said when he returned to his office.

"Do you?"

"No."

"I just wanted to see the lying little creep scared shitless for two minutes."

"It's funny how easy it often is to make out a case against someone if you put your mind to it, though," she said. "Plenty of circumstantial evidence against Jim."

He thought, as so often these past twenty-four hours, of Laura. What did the evidence against her amount to? A history of dead husbands; an emotionally impaired daughter who was no longer even below the age of consent and might have given her virginity voluntarily to any passing oaf; a little too much alcohol in the dead man's bloodstream with a pathologist who would not be prepared to swear on oath that it must have poleaxed him?

He could imagine getting up in a court of law and explaining how a bolting and terrified pony had been the key to the case, an event he had not personally witnessed. The Defense would have crucified him. If only she had been prepared to lie to him, to deny it to his face. He would have been only too happy to accept her word.

"Jim may have taken me in in a lot of ways," he went on, "but I can't see him sneaking around at night with a can of petrol and a rag, can you? And it's true that he didn't have any transport so how would he have got up to Hopcliff that night, to Glebe Street?" Nick dismissed Humbleby from his mind. "Let's put our heads together and go over everything we've got." He stood up and began to write on his whiteboard with a red pen which smelled strongly of chemicals. It carried a warning not to sniff it, but it had never done anything for him.

"The arsonist obviously had transport of some sort," Shirley said, "nothing too obtrusive, probably a car or a van—"

"A van. Yes." The possibly orange van with the possibly white markings which might have been seen parked by the telephone box that night. Something hovered in the back of his mind but wouldn't quite make it into his consciousness. It had something to do with Wayne's kite. He concentrated on the kite, on that blue and yellow canvas butterfly, on something Martha Greene had said in her whiny voice when she first answered the door to him.

"Motive?" he said.

"Revenge, presumably."

"So we're looking at someone with children of his own who's not satisfied with our efforts and is taking the law into his own hands."

"Jim wasn't far wrong when he spoke of a lynch mob."

So, he had What and Where and When and Why and How. Only Who still eluded him. Wayne and his kite. Wayne flying his kite in the park, high over the pond. No. That wasn't where he'd been to fly his kite that night.

Shirley was speaking again but he shushed her. The kite. Wayne coming up Cliff Walk with the kite and saying . . . what? That it was his birthday present. Yes. But something more.

"It came today on the van from the catalog!"

Martha, with no money to spare, bought from the mail-order catalog on the never-never. Martha, standing in the doorway, confused, expecting someone else. "I thought you was the delivery van, from the catalog!"

Martha grumbling: "They come later all the time."

Deborah Tyson: "I have to buy things I could get cheaper at the supermarket or from the catalogue."

Now he knew where he had heard that voice before—the one on the telephone at Mrs. Tyson's, the one on the 999 recording. He had heard it recently in the park.

"I've got a job, evenings, driving a van, delivering things."

"Who's Daddy's little sweetheart, then?"

Steve Clayton.

He jumped to his feet. "Steve Clayton."

"Who?"

Nick explained. "I want to talk to him. Come on."

The telephone rang. In the street, sirens seared into action. Nick crossed to the window and looked out. Two red fire engines raced past the police station and crossed the bridge, heading south.

"CID." Shirley answered the telephone. "WDS Walpole speaking." She listened for about a minute, said, "We're on our way," then hung up.

"It seems the spirit of Arturo Bottone isn't happy to rest in peace." She turned to Nick. "Colt's Head is on fire. Not the house, the stable—where he hanged himself."

■ ■ ■

After weeks of drought the moors were like tinder. If the fire brigade didn't control the blaze quickly, Nick thought, they could lose acres of wildlife and flora.

He could make out the fire on the horizon. It looked out of place in bright sunlight—it was for nights and overcast November days. Now it was competing vainly with the sun, its flames almost invisible against the blue sky. A pall of smoke on the other hand, spiraling upwards, was only too frighteningly visible. He revved his car hard and caught up with the fire engines as they slowed to negotiate the bends. Their sirens were no longer going, since there was no traffic to order out of the way, and they slinked like red dragons towards the blaze.

"Faster," he muttered, "faster."

When, at length, they reached Colts Head, he left his car just outside the yard so as not to impede the progress of any extra fire engines which might have been summoned from neighboring areas. By the time he and Shirley ran through the five-bar-gate the firemen were unrolling their hoses in their usual cool and controlled way. But their faces were grave. Some of them were clearing the yard, moving whisps of flammable material out of the danger zone, saturating the cobbles.

"The most we can do is stop it spreading to the house," the Chief Fire Officer called to Nick. "I think we should be safe enough there. But the stables are past saving. All that wood, straw, hay. Can you do something about getting those quadrupeds out of the paddock and off to a safe distance? I can't be responsible for them." Nick was about to comply when Felicity, her face streaked with soot, appeared from nowhere and hurled herself at him. "Uncle Nick!" Then he spotted Edwina standing in the yard behind her, staring up unmoved at the grey columns of smoke, Amy and Patience in either hand, Grace a few paces behind.

"Where's Laura, Felicity?" She didn't answer him, turned to point at the stable. "Oh no!" He shook the child by the shoulders. "What happened, Feckless, what happened?"

"What!" The Chief, overhearing, burst out. "You mean there's someone in there?"

"Mother!" Felicity began to sob like a baby. "Mummy! Mummy! Mummy!"

"There's no chance," the Chief said quietly to Nick. "No possible chance."

"We must do something, man. We can't just stand here."

"She'll have been overcome by fumes long ago. She's dead already. Trust me." Nevertheless he signaled his men, urging greater speed on them, and water soon began to fall in torrents on the skeleton of the stable roof and on the angry tongues of flame.

Marked police cars began to arrive on the scene, followed by ambulances. Nick ordered the uniformed PCs to move the frightened horses, and they began to evacuate the paddock with quiet efficiency, pressing blue and white incident tape into service to corral the animals inside a group of oaks. He admired their initiative.

"Come and sit down." He led Felicity to his own car and sat her comfortably in the passenger seat. He got in next to her and gave her his handkerchief. "Don't tell me. She saw the fire and went to try and save her beloved Golden Wonder."

Felicity shook her head, finding it hard to speak. "She

just went out . . . as usual. She said . . . she was taking Goldie for a hack . . . on her own. She often . . . did that. There was no . . . fire then. It was a few . . . minutes later. Edwina came in . . . and said . . . and said   ”

"It's okay. It's okay."

But it wasn't okay; it was never going to be okay again. He rocked her thin body against his as she became incoherent once more. Across the paddock he could see the firemen jumping clear as the stable roof finally collapsed, showering the yard with burning debris, which they hurried to put out with their stamping, heavy boots. Edwina still stood impassive, just watching, with Grace and Amy's heads now buried in her skirts. Patience, too young to comprehend, was crooning with excitement.

"Wait here a minute," he told Felicity. The children, fatherless and now motherless, must be got away. They should not be forced to see what he knew he must see when the fire died down. The Chief agreed that he might safely go into the house at this stage, and within fifteen minutes he had helped them pack their overnight bags and seen them safely piled into a patrol car with WPC Sally Ferris, who would take them to the children's home for the night.

It took several hours to control the fire. The house remained unscathed, but the stable was not even a shell. There was nothing left on that fateful site except charred beams, the ashes of the bales of straw which had provided such perfect kindling, and, huddled together in the far corner, what was left of an adult woman and a noble horse.

"Animals don't burn the way things do," the Chief Fire Officer remarked, "seventy percent water, you see. Even so, it'll be dental records for a definite ID on this one." Nick made no reply and the Chief added kindly, "It's not

quite as bad as you'd think to look at it. The smoke over-
comes them very quick. They don't know what's happening
at the end."

"No. I know. Thanks all the same."

The arsonist had done it at last, he thought. At the third
attempt, he had killed. And just when they had worked out
who he was, just hours too late.

"Come on," he called to Shirley. "Let's get to the station. I want to get a bit of backup and go and arrest Steve
Clayton for murder."

As they walked into the station less than half an hour later, the duty sergeant called out, "Inspector Burcombe
wants to talk to you, sir."

"Not now."

"He said it was urgent."

"And I said, not now!"

The sergeant shrugged. "I gave you the message." He
buzzed Nick and Shirley through the locked door and they
headed for the stairs.

"Inspector Trevellyan." A familiar voice hailed them
from behind before they were half way up. It sounded
pleased with itself.

"Not now, Burcombe."

"Suit yourself. I thought you'd like to know I arrested
your arsonist this morning."

"I matched up a name from our records with one on my
list of people buying cans of petrol," he said, as they followed him meekly down the stairs. "He's got a red van

with white stripes along it—pretty much like that bloke said—delivers stuff for Cronan's Mail Order all over the valley, in the evenings."

"Yes, I know," Nick said.

"People are used to seeing him about and don't think nothing of it, even at night."

"No, I know."

"He can go up to people's front doors carrying bags and packages and nobody turns a hair."

"I know."

"And a little girl he thinks the sun shines out the bum of. Hates these porn merchants like poison."

"Yes, I know."

"Got a juvenile record as long as your arm, too. I keep telling you, Nick: Once a villain, always a villain."

"Yes, you do keep telling me that," Nick agreed. He wondered at the madness, the hatred, which left a petty criminal like Steve Clayton now staring in the eye a life sentence for murder.

"He's admitted it, all of it," Burcombe said. "Tyson's and Greene's."

"Just like that?"

"Oh, you needn't look at me like that. I didn't lean on him; I didn't have to. He coughed easily enough, like I had any real evidence or anything!"

"You had no business questioning him at all," Nick pointed out. "That's CID's job."

"Well you weren't here, and no one seemed to know where you'd got to. I couldn't just leave him in the cell for hours without questioning him."

"Hours?" Shirley said.

"How many hours?" Nick asked sharply.

"I brought him in in the middle of the morning, not long after ten."

Nick and Shirley looked at each other. "Then how could he have been out setting fire to Colt's Head late this morning?" she said.

"That's what I'd like to know."

"He didn't say anything about Colt's Head," Burcombe put in, puzzled. "Why? What's happened?"

Nick didn't answer but wheeled round and headed back the way they had come. He checked the record kept by the custody sergeant, which confirmed that Burcombe had brought Clayton in just after ten that morning and that he had been either in the cells or in the interview room ever since.

"See," Burcombe said. He opened the peep hole in the door of cell number three and stood aside to let Nick take a look. Steve Clayton sat glumly on the bench opposite.

"He's all yours," Burcombe said. "He's been cautioned. He don't want a solicitor. Proud of his handiwork, he is. You will let me know if you want any more real police work doing, won't you?" He walked off, laughing.

"Bloody man," Shirley said. "We'll never hear the end of it."

Nick was barely listening. The fire at Colt's Head that morning had not been part of the arson pattern, come to think of it. It didn't match the others; it was a daytime attack. It could only be the deliberate act of a woman who could no longer live with what she had become. Was it characteristic that she should kill her favorite horse too, like some ancient pharaoh having all his servants buried alive to wait on him in the other world? He couldn't be sure, no longer felt that he had known her well enough to judge.

And Edwina? Standing there without visible emotion as the mother who had sent her away from home in punishment for her stepfather's crime died so horribly. Would that be the last straw for that splintered little mind?

"You want to try having kids of your own before you come over all sanctimonious." Steve Clayton spoke loudly and distinctly into the tape recorder. Neither Nick nor Shirley had any trouble recognizing the speaker from the 999 call now, and a voice print would soon confirm it.

"It's in the papers every day: kids abducted, interfered with, left dead in a ditch. Black magic and satanic rituals and I don't know what. Sheila don't hardly dare read the papers any more, not since Karen was born."

Nick could not interrupt the flow of this jumbled reasoning.

"Kids messed about with by their own parents. Fathers knocking seven bells out of them. Teachers touching up the infants. It's disgusting. And what happens when you lot catch up with them? Eh? I'll tell you. They get a fine, like fucking Tyson, or a couple of years inside like fucking Crick. Hanging's too good for them. They should be castrated."

He jabbed his finger at Nick to drive home his point. "If you won't do nothing about it, then we will. The parents. We'll take the law into our own hands and see that they get an eye for an eye like it says in the Bible. See. And I'm gonna stand up and say all this in court. I'll make them hear me. I want to see justice done. Not legal mumbo-jumbo and getting off on a technicality and 'not enough evidence' and clever-clever barristers. Justice, that's what I'm on about."

"Didn't you know there was a small boy living at the house where Crick was staying?" Nick asked. "That he could easily have been killed in the fire? What did you think that kite was for? For Mrs. Greene to play with? But you didn't think, did you? You just lashed out. And you call that Justice!"

"What about Colt's Head?" Shirley said.

"Eh? What about it?"

"Bottone's house. There was a fire there today." Both police officers watched Clayton closely. He looked genuinely bewildered.

"He was dead, the dago. Hanged himself. First decent thing he ever done in his life, I shouldn't wonder. Why should I torch his place?"

Why indeed, Nick thought?

"How long have I got to stay in this dump?" Clayton said. "That other copper made me take Karen to my sister's. Sheila'll be frantic if we aren't there when she gets home from work."

"You're staying here until I say otherwise," Nick said. "Your wife's been notified. You should think yourself lucky you're not facing a murder charge."

Steven Clayton was very lucky indeed, he reflected, that Burcombe had turned up to arrest him when he did. He couldn't hope for a better alibi than he had for the fire at the stable. Although no doubt the investigation would show a different *modus operandi,* Clayton might still have had trouble convincing a jury that he hadn't baked Laura Bottone alive.

7

It had been, more or less, the perfect murder.

As Nick sat with Alison on the terrace after supper a few nights later, he knew it would be a long time, perhaps many months, before he could get these last three weeks into perspective.

"Should I have minded my own business?" he burst out.

"What's that?" She put down the novel she was reading and looked at him with affection. "Did you say something?"

"I was the only one not willing to accept that suicide verdict. It would have breezed through the Coroner's inquest without an eyebrow being raised. It still will. But I had to stick my oar in."

"Well, of course you did."

"His death was, in a sense, no more than the revenge of his victims." He ground a sleepy wasp out between cup and saucer without mercy.

"You had a soft spot for Laura, didn't you?" she said. "She found one of those rare chinks in your armor."

"Yes. It wasn't anything that could threaten us, though, you and me."

"No, I know." She hesitated. "It's strange but I've never asked you—"

"What?"

"When Aidan was murdered and you thought for a while that I might have done it. Supposing for a moment that I had."

"Yes?"

"Would you have charged me?"

"If I had enough evidence, without a second thought."

"Perhaps that's why I've never asked."

"If you had done it, you wouldn't have been that enticing, delectable, infuriating Alison Hope I was already falling in love with. Murderers are not like other people. Murderers are not lovable, not to me."

They sat in silence while she mused on what he had said. "No more than the revenge of his victims. What about Edwin Rutherford? Is he to be condemned without trial too? And others?"

"How do you mean?"

"His mysterious car crash. An accident, just as Bottone's death was to be suicide. Might it not be that Laura had got the taste for murder—had started to see it as a rational answer to any problem or obstacle she encountered?"

"You're right," he said. "I can't allow myself the Natural Justice argument if I won't allow it to Steve Clayton."

"What's happening about him?"

"I've not opposed bail." Let him have a few weeks at home with the child he adored before being separated from her, perhaps for years.

"Was that my interference again?" he asked. Had the fright he had given him on the telephone that afternoon and the frustration of having his other calls intercepted pushed him into taking more concrete action? Might he otherwise have spent his anger in verbal abuse? Had Nick's visit to Crick led him straight to that poor inadequate old man?

245

"You can't take the blame for everything upon your shoulders," she told him gently. "Not for the wrongs of the whole world, Nick."

He took an envelope out of his briefcase. "You haven't seen this yet."

This was a preview of a newspaper article which he had received in the post that day—the first of Humbleby's promised offcuts.

"LYNCH-MOB JUSTICE," it shouted at him. "INSPECTOR NEGLECTS ARSON ATTACKS TO PURSUE PRIVATE VENDETTA."

Reg hadn't seen it yet, either, and would be apoplectic when he did. Not to mention the ACC (Admin). Naturally, it would be his fault.

"I feel so helpless," he said. "I can do nothing to preserve Ianthe from a slow and lonely death, nothing to help Wayne Greene and his useless mother—"

"You're due some leave. Ask her if we can take him for a few days out during the summer holidays: museums, art galleries, the cinema—show him something of our world."

"That's not a bad idea. Darling Alison, how practical you are." And he knew that there were other people looking out for Wayne too—good, caring men like Peter Walters.

The Tysons were gone, their damaged house up for sale in an already depressed market. The Bottone girls were in foster care until arrangements could be made for their future. The horses, even Felicity's adored Brimstone, had to be sold. Edwina had followed her original plan and left for Lambourn without a backward glance. Then there was Lucy's picture-book cottage at High Wind, featured on the lists of every estate agent in the valley. Everyone was on the move. It made him feel unsettled.

So, he asked himself, should he have left well alone, for his own peace of mind? Should he hold himself responsible for Laura's death? He could only answer as he had answered Lucy the week before: that there was only one way to live your life and that was by facing up to the truth and coming to terms with it.

"It wouldn't have been right," Alison said, following the path of his thought. "For another man, perhaps, my darling, but not for you."

You were free now. You were where you wanted to be all day long: with horses, mucking out, cleaning tack—you'd never minded those dirty jobs—going on the early-morning rides across the Berkshire Downs, watching the mist lift over the distant hills. You had left it all behind you and were making a new life, free of your history. You worked hard and slept soundly; there were no more dreams. You were not afraid any more.

One day you would be a jockey. One day you would be a champion and you would be loved and looked-up-to. Here you were one of the lads with no one to threaten you. You could join in their jokes, even their rough and tumble. Girls had to be able to take it and to dish it out too. Here your mind and your body could be one again. Next week you were going to your first race meeting: an evening meeting at Windsor, as Alpha Bravo's traveling lad.

You were sorry about your little half-sisters, since you loved them, especially Felicity—bless her—who thought she was so much cleverer than you were and believed so readily that it had been her own idea to kill him; but they were part of history and must be forgotten. They would survive, now that she was dead.

It was a shame about Goldie—he had deserved a better fate—but you could hardly have brought him out of that funeral pyre and left her shut up in there alone to die.

Could you?